ᵀʰᵉ ARREST

ALSO BY JONATHAN LETHEM

NOVELS

The Feral Detective
Gun, with Occasional Music
Amnesia Moon
As She Climbed Across the Table
Girl in Landscape
Motherless Brooklyn
The Fortress of Solitude
You Don't Love Me Yet
Chronic City
Dissident Gardens
A Gambler's Anatomy

NOVELLAS

This Shape We're In

SHORT STORY COLLECTIONS

The Wall of the Sky, the Wall of the Eye
Kafka Americana (with Carter Scholz)
Men and Cartoons
How We Got Insipid
Lucky Alan and Other Stories

The ARREST

JONATHAN LETHEM

atlantic · *fiction*

First published in the United States in 2020 by Ecco,
an imprint of HarperCollins Publishers Ltd, New York.

Published in trade paperback in Great Britain in 2020 by
Atlantic Books, an imprint of Atlantic Books Ltd.

10 9 8 7 6 5 4 3

A CIP catalogue record for this book is available
from the British Library.

Trade paperback ISBN: 978 1 83895 216 7
E-book ISBN: 978 1 83895 218 1

Printed in Great Britain by TJ Books Limited

Atlantic Books
An imprint of Atlantic Books Ltd
Ormond House
26–27 Boswell Street
London
WC1N 3JZ

www.atlantic-books.co.uk

For Anna

When you think about it, mostly, a cage is air—
So what is there
to be afraid of?
A cage of air. Baudelaire said
Poe thought America was one giant cage.
To the poet, a nation is one big cage.
And isn't the nation mostly filled with air?
Try to put a cage around your dream.
The cage escapes the dream.
I see it streak and stream.

—Sandra Simonds, *Atopia*

I.

TUESDAY

1.

FROST HEAVES

THIS ROAD IS LAID ON by the land's dictation. A horse path once and again, it isn't smoothed or straightened, routered through the hills. It climbs and collapses, adopts their shape. Here, you might not see something coming until it is upon you. Should there be word of a thing traveling furiously, fair enough. Be patient. What wends toward your town gets there when it will.

Do the hairs on your neck rise? Take a look. Much exists unseen. For instance, the crows in the canopy—you hear them, but can't pick them out. Mostly, you'll want to look where you're going, watch your step, on the irregular, undermined asphalt. A scattering of—is it acorns? Buckshot shells? Not those, not anymore. Scat, perhaps. At the road edge, the low walls, piles of cleared fieldstone. The deer are back, or never were gone. A question of where your eye lands.

Beyond these towns, the road slaloms south, deep and crooked from the mainland, into the peninsula, then across two causeways, now derelict. Vein through the meat of the old land, the road finds its finish on the main street of the fishing enclave on the southernmost of the two islands dangling from the peninsula's tip, into the Atlantic. A lobster town, its piers were for a half century partly overtaken by galleries and restaurants, a stand selling ice cream loaded in chocolate-dipped cones. Anyone might have gone there, just once, and complained about tourists. It's a fishing village again. Two hours by horse or bicycle to the quarry towns.

Too far to go. Forget those lobstermen, who rarely appear. It's the others, those on horseback, calling themselves the Cordon, who are essential to anticipate, defer to, avoid. They guard the south and west perimeters, the ways out by land. To escape this peninsula now, there's only the sea. Not your thing. Stay with the road.

The rusted yellow highway warning sign reading FROST HEAVES presents a syntactic puzzle. A verb itself frozen. Was there one particular heave, a buckling in an otherwise smooth surface, that once dictated placement of the warning at this spot? The whole roadway surface is heaves now. Someone with a bullet to spare, long ago, shot the metal sign. Forever a surprise the bullet passed through, didn't get stuck.

Maybe Frost is in fact a person, that poet we studied in high school. Frost heaves into the mind. His road diverged, ours doesn't. Though, really, isn't any road you could follow in either of two directions divergent enough to begin with?

2.

THE LAKE OF TIREDNESS

JOURNEYMAN WAS ON THE ROAD this day, north out from the village, to do one of his two regular jobs. Making rounds, by foot, because his bicycle needed repair. He wasn't a horseman, though he could ride one in a pinch, he imagined. Had done it once or twice at summer camp, in the Poconos. It wasn't as though much he'd learned in the first part of his life had turned out to be applicable in this, the second. This life wasn't the one he thought he'd be living.

It was Journeyman's job to visit the man who lived at the Lake of Tiredness. To bring the man food and other supplies, like candles and hand-spun dental floss. Though really it had proven easy enough just to leave packages at the top of the road; the prisoner would pace up and retrieve them. Prisoner of sorts. There was nothing keeping the man from continuing beyond that point, the juncture where the path to his lakeside cabin joined the peninsula's main thorough-fare. Nothing besides a kind of agreement between the man and the town, that he should be exiled or retired there. The man, whose name was Jerome Kormentz, was quite elderly. Where would he go?

The road to the Lake of Tiredness was long overgrown, sprung grasses concealing the old gravel tire beds from the center and sides, an entirely successful comb-over. In the shade of dense foliage the air was cool and dry, on a hot bright day, outstanding in every way. Journeyman would remember this later. Some of the crows had followed him from the main road. Or maybe it was other crows. He wasn't that dedicated a watcher of crows.

The path widened to a clearing. A lawn that had once long ago been diligently mowed now rippled with the same grasses that infilled the gravel beds, and voluntary saplings that would, if left untended, reclaim this land as woods. Everything here wanted to be woods. As a city child visiting New England he'd once taken the pastures, rimmed by dense trees, as a natural formation. A pleasing alternation of the dense and spare, the shadowed and sunlit. Now he'd come to understand that every cleared place in Maine recorded a massive human undertaking, likely by some eighteenth- or nineteenth-century farmer and his neighbors. A quiet war with the growth, once won, now mostly lost again.

At the bottom, the cabin on the shore, a dock extended a brief distance into the water. The Lake of Tiredness was actually a large pond, this had been explained to him once. A matter of outflow and inflow, or lack thereof.

Kormentz came up from the house. Kormentz did this every time, though there was no schedule to the visits, offering a hearty greeting: arms outthrust, hairy-knobbed wrists exposed from his kimono, extending for a handclasp. Charging uphill despite the fact that he was old and his visitor was, if not young, younger. Middle-aged. And despite the fact they'd then turn and descend together to the cabin.

When he saw Jerome Kormentz's face, Journeyman had to adjust to how old Kormentz had gotten, though he'd known him only five years. The effect wore off quickly. Journeyman would later reflect on how he'd rehearsed this perception this particular day, with Kormentz, because he was to apply it just hours later to a different person, one he'd had no notion of ever seeing again.

3.

TIME AVERAGING

THAT WAS JOURNEYMAN'S NAME FOR it: Time Averaging. It wasn't a complicated idea. A thing that happens when you first lay eyes on someone you've known a long time, but whom you only see intermittently. A thing you do to their faces, with your mind. Time Averaging could also happen if you knew a child, or a teenager—if they were your nephew or niece, say.

It worked like this: You saw them. They appeared shockingly old. Or in the case of the child, startlingly grown. You found time to wonder: Where did the time go? Am I old, too? Were they managing the same confusion, even as they smiled and said how great you look? Then you'd fix them in your mind, using Time Averaging. Your mind held a cache of earlier versions, and you'd merge them to make the person continuous with the earlier rendition. You located their beauty and unspoiledness, and smoothed it up into the picture. If the person was truly elderly, like Jerome Kormentz, you'd recuperate them, to a degree. If a teenager, you'd find the younger child still lurking in their face.

The persons for whom we perform the most remarkable acts of Time Averaging, Journeyman tended to think, were lovers, former and present. Of course. Lovers and siblings. In his present life, he found himself Time Averaging his sister nearly every day, despite the briefness of the intervals.

If you'd told Journeyman, before the Arrest, that he'd come to a life in which he saw his sister nearly every day, he'd have been bewildered at the suggestion.

Time Averaging wasn't a difficult operation, in Journeyman's view. In fact, it was impossible not to perform it. Journeyman supposed it was also a thing done to oneself in the mirror, though this seemed to cheapen the theory. He wasn't interested in mirrors, these days. The striking thing wasn't the Time Averaging itself, but the existence of the tiny interval in which it hadn't yet occurred. That moment where we see things as they are.

Journeyman suspected we also did this to the world. It must be the case.

4.

THE PILLOW BOOK OF
JEROME KORMENTZ

JOURNEYMAN WAS OF AVERAGE HEIGHT, but Kormentz made him feel tall. Kormentz had always reminded Journeyman of a fishperson, his eyes goggled, his perpetually smiling lips pursed, lower lip a valentine, his thin hair streamed almost invisibly back to cover his scalp. As Kormentz aged, this impression deepened, despite the effect of the Time Averaging. Maybe someday the resemblance would climax and he'd leap into the Lake of Tiredness, shiver into goldfish form, and vanish. Kormentz's mystical bent made it seem possible.

"Good morning, Sandy!" Journeyman's given name was Alexander Duplessis. Mostly these days he was called Sandy. His family nickname, it had been propagated locally by his sister, before he could intervene.

"Hello, Jerome."

"Storyteller, tell me a story." A standard provocation from Kormentz.

"I'm not your storyteller or anyone's, Jerome."

"No, you're the butcher, now. Did you bring me a lean chop? A portion of somebody's beloved lamb, named Freckle or Daisy?" He scurried alongside Journeyman as they moved toward his deck.

"I brought you some pig. Good enough for soup."

"But what's the pig's name? A he- or a she-pig? Did you slaughter her yourself? Have you grown more accustomed to it? You know how I'm starved for names, Sandy. Something for my brain-soup. I can live without the people if you'll just give me the names. Then I'll invent the people for myself."

"Here's a story," Journeyman said. "Ed Waltz got a tractor to move a few dozen yards across his field, using human waste mixed with the used oil from Mike Raritan's deep fryer. He thinks that might be the recipe." The people of the Cordon had functional motorcycles. Nobody knew the secret of their fuel, except that their rides smelled like shithouses.

"Ed and Mike, that's a start. How about Sarah and Jennifer and Penny? How about Susan? What can you tell me about Susan? Has anyone new moved into the yurt?"

"I'm not sure what you're talking about. If it's the Susan I'm thinking of, she's one of those who left."

"Pity."

"Here's what I have for you." Journeyman unslung his backpack, a relic of the before. It read TELLURIDE FILM FESTIVAL 2020 on the straps, though faded almost to illegibility. He'd gotten it as a freebie. There'd been a backpack like it, each full of Criterion Blu-rays and other swag, waiting in each guest's hotel room. Had others been subsequently stained, as this one had, by rinsings in the blood of fresh-slaughtered ducks and sheep, or by lard-smeared mason jars of new-rendered pig parts, such as Journeyman unloaded now? He also fished out a rubber-banded bundle of carrots—he retrieved the rubber band for future use—and some loose spring onions and garlic scapes. "There's a good soup to be had here," he said. "Especially if you've been gathering mushrooms."

"There's a book I need you to find for me, Sandy."

"What book?"

"*The Pillow Book of Sei Shōnagon*. Ancient Japanese text, tenth or eleventh century, I think."

"*Pillow Book?*" Journeyman didn't like the sound of it. "Like that Doris Day movie, what's it called? Oh, *Pillow Talk*."

"Sandy, you're a philistine. It's one of the classic early literary texts. The author was a lady at the emperor's court. She recorded her impressions toward the end of her life, with no expectation of publication. Or perhaps she had one sly eye on posterity. Years ago I memorized great swaths of it—alas, all gone now. I do recall it was broken into these marvelous categorical lists, like 'Things that should be large,' or 'Things that give a pathetic impression,' or 'Things that make one nervous.'"

Jerome Kormentz aloft on one of his jags: this was a thing that made Journeyman nervous. It made him feel answerable, even if there was no one else around. He was bothered by Kormentz's constant invocation of "Eastern" stuff. It was with Eastern stuff that Kormentz had beguiled the two teenage girls at Spodosol Ridge Farm. The actions that had led, eventually, to this cozy exile. Journeyman himself had a kind of tone deafness when it came to Eastern stuff, or at least to the Eastern stuff spouted by Westerners who fancied themselves enlightened. He did pine for sushi restaurants, and for Wong Kar-wai movies, and older Japanese samurai movies, by Kurosawa and Kobayashi. Some of these remained shelved, tantalizingly, at the town library, where he supposed he'd go soon, to try to find Kormentz his *Pillow Book*. Not that any of the local tinkerers had time or inclination to spare for rigging up a prototype bicycle-powered or human-waste-fueled DVD or Blu-ray player.

"I'm writing my own version," he added into Journeyman's silence. "*The Pillow Book of Jerome Kormentz*. It has the same odds of lasting as Sei Shōnagon's, but you never know."

"Does it rhyme?"

"No," Kormentz said. "Why do you ask that?"

"Aren't most things that last really some kind of song? Like *The Odyssey*? And they shot that Chuck Berry number out into space." Talk with Kormentz often plumbed regions of bizarre fact Journeyman had no idea remained relocatable within him. "Never mind. What's your *Pillow Book* about?"

"Read Sei Shōnagon's before you bring it to me and you'll understand. Just the purest impressions of life as it is lived, without apology."

It was clear where this led. "I'll take a look," Journeyman said, sourly. He'd unpacked the last of the vegetables now, and the mason jar of goat milk yogurt his sister always set aside for Kormentz. Nothing kept him. Other days he might linger to talk, but not today.

"I was always a loving person," Kormentz blithered. "Everyone knew that. I believed it was sweet and kind, a light I was spreading at the Farm. I love women, Sandy. I made them feel irresistible. Everyone knew I did a little touching, a hand at the small of the back—"

Journeyman had heard it before: the small of the back. Kormentz still luxuriated in his moment of disaster. This had been the cause, as much as his crime, of his removal to the Lake of Tiredness—the fact that he couldn't quit talking about it.

5.

THE ARREST, SUCH AS JOURNEYMAN UNDERSTOOD IT

WITHOUT WARNING EXCEPT EVERY WARNING possible it had come: the Arrest. The collapse and partition and relocalization of everything, the familiar world, the world Journeyman had known his whole life.

The future, that is to say, announced itself. The future always already present but distributed unequally, like everything else—like bread, talent, sex, like peepal, neem, aloe, and those other plants that give off oxygen at night, like the rare spodosol-rich ground for which Journeyman's sister's farming collective was named. The Arrest produced itself as a *now* already *past*. Like a time capsule unearthed.

This was confusing. It should be confusing. Did Journeyman understand the world into which he'd been born—its premise, its parameters, its plot? No. So, why should he grasp how it had changed?

How even to say when the Arrest began? The question was when had it gained your attention. Plenty flew under the radar. Biodiversity halved? That made an impression, barely. Polar ice and Miami drowned? Terrible, yet also too big to take personally. One day Journeyman noticed reports of a new tick-borne disease. Once you'd been bitten, cow meat made your throat close up. No more American Wagyu tomahawk steak for two, black on the outside, red within. People joked uneasily. Were the new ticks an eco-terrorist hack? On television, someone said that the turning point had been when in 1986 the president had removed the solar panels from the White House. Then again, someone else said the turning point had been when St. Paul's epistle had been delivered to the Romans and ignored. You could debate this shit forever.

But not on television, not any longer. Here the Arrest at last commanded Journeyman's attention. He sat up and noticed the death of screens. They died not all at once, the screens, but in droves, like creatures of the warmed ocean, like those hundreds of manatees washing ashore the same day in Boca Grande who, just weeks before, Journeyman had found uncompelling, and deleted from his feed. He'd unfollowed the manatees. No hard feelings.

Television died first. Television contracted a hemorrhagic ailment, Ebola or some other flesh-melting thing. The channels bled, signals fused, across time as well as virtual space, a live Rod Serling *Playhouse 90* teleplay broadcast from 1956 sputtering into last agonized life and expiring in the middle of episodes of season two of *Big Little Lies*. The Vietnam War came back, and *Family Ties* too. Until these boiled and melted along with the rest.

The Gmail, the texts and swipes and FaceTimes, the tweets and likes, these suffered colony collapse disorder. Each messenger could no longer chart its route to the hive, or returned only to languish in the hive, there to lose interest in its labors, whether worker or drone. All at once, the email quit producing honey.

So many other ecologies depended on the pollinations, the goings-between of the now-fatigued drones and workers. Without them, nothing worked. Air-conditioning units stalled, planes fell from the sky. The honey of emails and texts had been the glue holding the world together, it appeared. Now the smart devices all evidenced wasting disease. They had to be put out to a level pasture to let them graze out the last part of their lives. There they crumpled to their knees, starved, incapable of grazing.

People kept on swiping at the phones and mashing at the keyboards. Some tried giving the voice-activated devices mouth-to-mouth resuscitation. Some proposed fixes or work-arounds. Those more mystically minded placed phones or remotes beneath their pillows at night or built shrines in which to surround their devices with crystals, hoping to spark them from their silence. Others, like Journeyman, merely kept glancing at the screens that had gone dark, and also sat periodically weeping. Some, like Journeyman, needed eventually to be given a mug of herbal tea while someone else hid their inert former electronic playthings.

A solar flare?

Eco-terror? Terror-terror? Species revenge? The Revolution?

Had Journeyman's world jumped the shark?

The stars didn't go out, one by one.

The U.S. wasn't replaced with a next thing. It was replaced by wherever one happened to be. The place one happened to reside at the moment of the Arrest, which after a fitful start had come overnight. Did they even call it the Arrest elsewhere? Journeyman counseled himself to be done with such speculation. BE HERE NOW; WHEREVER YOU GO, THERE YOU ARE; ALL POLITICS ARE LOCAL: every bumper sticker had come true at once, even as the cars slumped sidelong from the roads to make way for other means of transit. Every tank seemed sugared by the same prankster, the gasoline turned to a thing that inched from the pump nozzles like molten flourless cake.

Guns worked for months, for nearly a year after the initial Arrest. Then died too, souring like milk. The bullets no longer even blew up if you shattered them with a hammer—Journeyman had seen it tried.

Goodbye to gasoline and bullets and to molten flourless cake. Goodbye to coffee. To bananas and Rihanna, to Father John Misty,

to the Cloud, to news feeds full of distant core meltdowns, to manatees and flooded cities and other tragedies Journeyman had guiltily
failed to mourn. Hello instead to solar dehydrators, rooftop rain
collectors, to beans, kale, and winter squash. To composting toilets
and humanure, to a killing cone, feather plucker, and evisceration
knife. Say hello to chasing a screaming duck into a pond to drag
back to the killing cone. To being the butcher's sluice boy.

Had Journeyman known that barns were traditionally painted
red to disguise the bloodstains? He hadn't. Journeyman had been
playing catch-up since the Arrest, cribbing from field guides, farmer's almanacs, seed catalogs, old Michael Pollan paperbacks. Could
he become a man of the soil in mid-life? No, he was too old a dog for
that trick. The peninsula was choked with expert organic farmers,
lured here by the locavore movement. His sister was one of them.

That's why Journeyman worked with the butcher, Augustus
Cordell, sluicing bloody steel tables, retrieving offal and caul for
Victoria's sausage-making. Victoria's creations—her summer sausage, her hard salami, her black pudding—were prized by the whole
peninsula, but also used as barter with the people of the Cordon. As
it turns out, therefore, Journeyman could wish he'd been carrying
a packet of them in his Telluride Film Festival backpack five minutes later that same morning, after climbing the lake's overgrown
driveway, back to the main road.

6.

AN OLD FRIEND

AT FIRST JOURNEYMAN THOUGHT IT was bees or deerflies, a kind of humming, as he pushed out of the canopy, onto the sun-mottled asphalt. He mistook the humming for the bee-loud glade. This day was still weirdly perfect. Journeyman, freed of Kormentz's monologue, was interested to search for the book the prisoner had requested. It had caught his imagination. Journeyman had a little crush, too, on the woman who'd moved into the library—it made an excuse to visit there.

It wasn't bees. A contingent from the Cordon was on the roadway. Their humming resolved into something more irregular, the guttering of their night-soil engines, as they approached. Journeyman distinguished the sound a minute before the riders appeared, hovering into view over the roadway's contour. Two shit-Harleys. Behind them, two other men, on horseback. The four were an advance team for something else. Some stormhead rumbling farther back on the road.

Journeyman stood blinking as they dismounted. He knew one of the riders, who called himself Eke. Was this short for Ezekiel, or Ekediah, or some other longer name? Journeyman didn't know. Eke might have been in his late twenties. His hair was slicked back and cut stylishly high on both sides, though he wore the stalactite beard of a Cordon elder.

"Mr. Duplessis." It was the way of the Cordon to address members of Journeyman's community formally, or mock-formally. Eke, for one, spoke with impunity to men decades older than himself, or at least to Journeyman. He picked his nose in front of Journeyman too—evidence, if needed, that the formality in his address was more mock than otherwise.

"Hello, Eke."

"Just the man I wanted to see. Good piece of luck finding you on the road."

"It's good to see you too, Eke, but I wasn't expecting you. I haven't got anything." Journeyman still, at this point, imagined this might concern sausage, or other supplies.

"This isn't about nothing like that."

"No?"

"You're good with us, Mr. Duplessis. We wouldn't ask for more than's our fair share."

"What can I do you for?"

"We got a strange one for you. Comes with you and your sister's name attached. If your names hadn't got mentioned, I doubt we'd be here."

"I don't understand."

"Fellow came up our way in a kind of *car*." He waved behind him, at the road. The other men on the stopped motorcycles, and the two horses, including Eke's own, seemed to flicker their attention back the way they'd come as well, as if Eke had their sight lines tethered to his hand by invisible threads.

"A working car?"

Eke paused to shake his head, signifying something outside the box. "Not like one any of us ever seen. It's big. Kind of an armored car. A supercar, I guess you'd say." Later, Journeyman would reflect on how Eke's nomenclature stuck: *supercar*. Perhaps the inevitable term. "He won't come down from it, says he'll talk to Sandy Duplessis or Madeleine Duplessis only. He also knew the name of your sister's farm out there."

"You couldn't . . . get him out of his car?"

"Well, not if we didn't dynamite him out of it. Which, I can tell you, we were prepared to do, until he began shouting your name down. Like I said, it's been a puzzler. We're not afraid of him, mind you. Some proposed turning him back the way he came, but others felt we wouldn't mind taking a look at the operation of the thing, if we could get him down from it without dynamite. We thought you and your sister might want to at least give him a hearing before we made the call."

"Down?" Journeyman couldn't visualize this. Also, he was distracted by something he'd noticed: that two of the Cordon's men bore bandages on their limbs. One, a thick hump of gauze at the juncture of his shoulder and neck. Had they been in some kind of battle? Were these wounds acquired in wrangling this supercar? Or should Journeyman take their tales of periodically invading hordes more seriously than he had?

"He's seated up pretty high," said Eke. "You'll see." He glanced over his shoulder. Now Journeyman heard it and saw it. Not the car itself, which remained around a few bends and below a few rises. Just the rumbling cloud it raised, on a still and sunny afternoon. Eke appeared a bit rattled by the thing he'd been trying to describe, that thing coming.

What were Journeyman's feelings, at that immanence, that Tuesday when it first came, before it rounded into view? Was he rattled too?

Certainly. But something more. Journeyman felt an abject throb of who-he-used-to-be. Someone in a quote, unquote "supercar" had come bearing his name as his bona fides? Journeyman might be more than the town's emissary to the Lake of Tiredness and the

butcher's sluice boy. He might be an important person on this peninsula.

"This man—he really knew my name?" Surely, there was a trick
in this. The dust cloud grew nearer. Otherwise, time had stopped.
A crow moved from branch to branch, a blob of shadow on the sun-
daubed road. Journeyman could so easily have stayed longer banter-
ing with Jerome Kormentz, and missed this strange caravan rolling
through. Perhaps then Eke would have implicated whomever he'd
come across, instead of Journeyman.

"Your name, Mr. Duplessis. No mistaking that."

"Did he give his?"

Eke scratched deep into his beard with strong fingers. "Yes, he
did. Said Peter Todbaum. Said you'd know him."

7.

THE STARLET APARTMENTS, PART 1

WHEN HE AND PETER TODBAUM were twenty-four, and two years clear of Yale, he'd lost track of Todbaum for a short while.

This was in the time before Journeyman had been awarded his private nickname, let alone accepted its verdict.

Journeyman had been living in New York City, working as an assistant at FSG, writing short stories that no one wanted to publish, when Todbaum got back in touch. Todbaum had acquired an agent and was going to Hollywood. He wanted Journeyman with him, as co-writer on a stack of ideas he promised Journeyman he'd already developed and vetted with his representation, and which only needed Journeyman's hand. Journeyman, not William Goldman or Nora Ephron. Todbaum had a place picked out for them in Burbank, where they'd shack up and bash out treatments and it would be a great adventure, like Yale without all the pointless Yale stuff, and with a good deal more cocaine. Hearing it, Journeyman was sold. He was there in a heartbeat.

The place was the Starlet Apartments, a classic '30s two-story complex curled around a pool. Monthly rentals, with a motley assortment of long- and short-term occupants, plenty of empty apartments too. This was in Burbank, right under the shadow of the high-walled Warner Bros. lot. Todbaum joked that the place was named for its traditional use as a lunchtime casting couch liaison site, and his joke was likely right.

The two holed up there at the Starlet to bat out projects poolside and in the paltry second-floor suite they shared, with the AC cranked. At night, they drove to West Hollywood bars in Todbaum's father's cast-off BMW, where they drank shots of Jägermeister and tried to pick up women, many of whom were considerably older than they were. At this, they never once succeeded, nor did they mind. The young men were too full of themselves and their projects to mind. Todbaum's agent called every few days to ask how their work was coming along; he champed at the bit to get them into "good offices" as soon as the material was ready. And so, half the time, even at the bars, even blitzed on German digestif, they ignored their surroundings and continued to work, to brainstorm their notions for screenplays and television shows. They worked side by side in deck chairs while the complex's other young tenants tried to entice them into the pool.

Blitzed or hungover, Journeyman fastened himself to the task. In his mind, he and Todbaum were Billy Wilder and Charles Brackett, perhaps; Todbaum the bullshitter, Journeyman the hands on the keyboard. Todbaum would circle Journeyman where he sat, reeling out great fugues of self-infatuated improv, doing voices, abruptly changing lines or names of characters, forcing Journeyman to hurriedly xxxxxxx out endless lines on their Canon Typestar. Then Todbaum would jerk the pages from Journeyman's hands to scribble further emendations, or ball them up to toss into the suite's corners. They hammered out one whole script, a horror movie based on one of Journeyman's unpublished stories, and four or five long treatments, several of them broad, idiotic comedies pegged for stars of the day, Carrey or Martin or Murphy.

Their pet project, one of Todbaum's supply of "killer pitches," was a science fiction movie he called *Yet Another World*. This was a tale of alternate nightmare Earths. One was their own version of reality, the other an Orwellian techno-dystopia, a kind of cyberpunk extrapolation from the Cold War '50s, when the two worlds had bifurcated. The story began when the two worlds discover a portal that allows them to communicate, one with the other (the exact means of communication was unclear, a thing Todbaum relied on Journeyman to think up). *Yet Another World* was also a love story, with an impossible obstacle: a man from the dystopian cyberpunk world (Harrison Ford, probably, or Bruce Willis) would fall in love with a scientist from their world (Michelle Pfeiffer was Todbaum's pick; he thought she'd be hot in glasses).

Along with scripts and treatments, the two young men also hammered out what would be for two decades, with only minor interruptions, Journeyman's life situation. That was to say, Peter Todbaum talking and Journeyman typing, and eventually collecting a fair amount of money for it. For Jerome Kormentz hadn't been totally groundless to call Journeyman "storyteller." In that previous life, in the world before the Arrest, storytelling was the way Journeyman buttered his bread.

Todbaum and Journeyman sold none of what they made in the Starlet, though they did run those notions in and out of a great number of meetings. They excelled in near misses that may not have been near at all, involving follow-up conference calls and weeks of waiting, or requests for further work on spec that were rarely rewarded with more than a free coffee. Nonetheless, by the time their run was concluded, and Todbaum's agent's Rolodex exhausted, two things were apparent. The first was that Journeyman, the silent partner, the keyboard man, could bat out reams of more or less what was needed in this town, the fuel it all ran on, and that sooner or later he might be remunerated for it. Second, that Peter Todbaum had a different gift, for spinning rooms into a kind of visionary frenzy of promise on the pinwheel of his tongue, even if the rooms, in this early phase, quit spinning when he exited. More than one of the development executives the two met with joked to Todbaum, in so many words, "You should have my job!" Soon, he did. And Journeyman would spend the next decades working principally for him.

In the last of the five months the two men spent living at the Starlet, Journeyman's sister graduated college. Madeleine Duplessis had attended Baginstock College, on the coast of Maine, a boutique liberal arts college she'd chosen, perhaps, in order to avoid Journeyman's family's legacy school. She was just two years younger than her brother, a difference in age that had evaporated in the subsequent decades' atmosphere: her serious life and Journeyman's unserious one. Yet his role as the older sibling might have mattered still, back when she took up the invitation to visit Los Angeles, and to stay with her brother and Peter Todbaum at the Starlet.

Maddy had accepted, Journeyman understood, in order to avoid landing back at "home," on Fishers Island, the place where their parents had elegantly retired after shoving the kids off to college. Maddy had had enough of the Atlantic coast for a spell, perhaps. She'd majored in environmental science and oceanography, and had in her last year moved into a collective off-campus house dedicated to organic farming. She had no special purpose in Los Angeles, let alone in the entertainment industry, but what purpose was needed beyond curiosity, at twenty-two? And why shouldn't the two young writers want a tall attractive sister to accompany them into the West Hollywood nightlife, to make them appear less like losers?

Maddy had attained her full height. Or perhaps she'd been encouraged by her communal friends to straighten and not be ashamed of her full height. She was taller than their parents (who'd begun shrinking), and taller, too, than Journeyman, and Peter Todbaum, when he rose to greet her. She and Peter hadn't met during Journeyman's Yale years, and when she came through the door of the suite, her only luggage a hiker's backpack, dressed in a tank top and high-trimmed jean shorts, Journeyman felt Todbaum's instant excitement at her presence.

"Well, fuck me in the heart," he said. "Who's this long drink of water?" Todbaum used his Cary Grant voice for this. Todbaum was a capable vocal mimic, though he typically dialed up hoary movie stars that sounded, by now, like impressions of impressions: Peter Lorre, John Wayne, and so forth. Other times he used a chesty, bullying voice Journeyman didn't recognize, and which Todbaum explained was actually his father's. Once or twice, he'd japed in an uncanny impersonation of Journeyman's own voice, until Journeyman begged him to stop.

"Peter, Madeleine," Journeyman said now, as if at a freshman mixer.

"Well, how do you do?" said Todbaum. "From what the Sandman here told me, I was picturing a little mud-hippie. Some kind of hairy-ankled garden gnome." Todbaum was free with nicknames, and one of his for Journeyman was Sandman—a reworking of Journeyman's given name and a joke about how Journeyman would often conk out in the middle of parties, or during one of Todbaum's ceaseless sentences.

"A mud-hippie?" Maddy glanced at her brother. Journeyman recalled that he'd mentioned to Todbaum how Madeleine had cured herself of childhood ailments, including that of preppiness, through devotion to farming and the outdoors, to a macrobiotic diet and other alternative practices.

"Maybe there's a secret Dutch gene lurking in the frog family lineage, eh?" He also liked to riff on Journeyman's last name, Duplessis, and the suggestion that all of what he considered his pretensions— jazz, wire-rim eyeglasses, and red wine—were traces of French ancestry. "Someone must've took a walk on the Walloon side."

"Sorry?" said Madeleine, even as she came out of a brief embrace with Journeyman to offer her hand to Todbaum. He lifted it to his lips and, weirdly, sniffed it. Maddy pulled it free.

"You look fresh off the Prinsengracht Canal," he said. "Where's your bicycle?"

Maddy jostled back at him, a little. "Oh, it folds up small. I've got it right here in my pack."

Todbaum's manner of acknowledging this was to turn to Journeyman. "She walks, she talks, she—whaddayou frogs call it?—she *ripostes.*"

"Did my brother tell you I was mute?"

"He didn't prepare me in any way," said Todbaum.

"That's good, I wouldn't want him to. You'll just have to roll with the punches."

"Oh, I'll roll!" said Todbaum delightedly.

"Good," said Maddy, turning to Journeyman. "Can we get something to eat?"

What had Journeyman expected, introducing them? Not this— Todbaum's open drooling, his sister's "ripostes." His kid sister— hand-holding toddler, mutual confidante and whisperer, agonizing nightly violin-practicer, and stricken sufferer of childhood psoriasis and psoriatic arthritis. The hours she'd spent smoothing lotion onto her arms and legs, sunning in hopes of a solar cure, that teenage prisoner of sore flaking knees. Though they'd drifted somewhat, in high school, Maddy was lodged in Journeyman's somatic sense of himself. He felt as though the center of his chest might once have been fused to hers, as though they'd been separated conjoined twins with one multifarious heart.

Had Todbaum been aggressive with women at college? Todbaum, so far as Journeyman recalled, hadn't been any way in particular. He'd been a reveler, a sophomoric provocateur—not a lover at all. Or maybe he kept that part of his life hidden. Perhaps his provocations of Maddy, now, were a display for Journeyman's sake.

The rest of the night suggested so. The three went out to the Dresden and, after that initial flare of response, Todbaum back-burnered Maddy. The writers were caught up entirely in infatuation with their new toy, the science fiction movie. They drank and spun their pitch, and Maddy drank and watched. Three time zones behind, she tired early. The next morning, Todbaum appeared impatient to find her on the couch when he came out for morning coffee (the suite lacked a third bedroom), and seemed only grudgingly amused at their sibling familiarities.

The second night—out, again, at Todbaum's insistence, at the Dresden—she leaned across her drink and interrupted their talk. "You gave her the dull half."

Todbaum raised his eyebrows.

"Dull half of what?" said Journeyman.

"Your movie. *Yet Another World*. What, you thought I wasn't listening?"

"It doesn't have a dull half," her brother told her.

"Sure it does. The regular stuff—our world, I mean. All you guys talk about is the cyberpunk part, the dystopian part, where the *guy* comes from. But the part about our world, *you're* not even interested in it. It's like the whole thing just exists so he can have a girlfriend."

"Hey, look at our little story doctor," said Todbaum, suddenly alert to her. Or unconcealing an alertness he'd been veiling— Journeyman would need to wonder, later on.

"She's not just his girlfriend," Journeyman complained. "She's a scientist. They're, uh, equals."

"Right, okay," said Maddy. "A scientist of what?"

Neither had the answer to this.

"And her world sucks."

"It's our world."

"It's nobody's world. It's like *movie* world. A flat backdrop. Nobody's lived there since the 1950s, if they ever did."

"What would you suggest?" said Todbaum.

"I need another drink," said Maddy. She was through her second Blood and Sand, a dangerously dessert-like cocktail. Journeyman thought to protest, but said nothing. After Todbaum had provided a third round, she repeated, "It's flat."

"You said that."

"The actual world doesn't flatten for your convenience. It's a boring lie. That's why the other half of your movie is better. Put her world in motion too. Maybe an ecological catastrophe."

"Keep talking." This might have been Todbaum's motto for himself.

"Make her an environmental scientist. She's trying to save her reality, he's trying to save his. They're *both* under pressure. What did you call it? A ticking clock?"

Todbaum pointed his glass at Journeyman. "Maybe I bet on the wrong Duplessis. Because that's good."

Journeyman was silenced.

"You got your dystopia in my postapocalypse," Todbaum said. "You got your postapocalypse in my dystopia. Hey, these taste pretty good together! It's a Reese's Peanut Butter Cup meet-cute for two fucked-up worlds."

"Now you owe me a percentage," said Maddy.

"I owe you another drink, that's for sure."

"You can't buy me for the price of a Blood and Sand."

"Let's see how many it takes."

Journeyman didn't actually mind. He liked them to like one another, was happy to think he'd provided two-way ratification of a general okayness—it made him feel better about his own choices, and the chance his sister would provide his parents an encouraging report. What's more, the movie was better for her idea. The movie was suddenly great, as great as they'd thought it was before.

It was the third night Journeyman would spend a lifetime wondering whether he'd been meant to foresee and prevent. It happened before he knew it. The third night was a Friday. When the Starlet broke out in its usual half-assed pool revels, which Todbaum usually disdained, he surprised Journeyman by suggesting that they stay in.

There were some new faces, he said. A cutie or two. They wouldn't have to drink and drive for a change, only fall back into their rooms. Only later did Journeyman see how every part of this was congruent with Todbaum's scheme, assuming he'd formed it in advance.

Journeyman woke at four or five on a deck chair, his throat raw. Todbaum had poured liquor and pot not into Maddy—well, he'd likely done that too—but into Journeyman. And, from Journeyman, conspicuously withheld the cocaine. Journeyman's hair was stiff and rank with chlorine, though at some point he'd gotten back into his tee and jeans. He'd either made out with one of the not-terribly-cuties, or tried to and only kissed and fumbled. Todbaum's power of suggestion over him was awful. Alone now, he went upstairs. The suite was locked, Journeyman's key inside. He rattled at the door, imagining his sister would hear him from the couch, but no. He didn't ponder this, but instead staggered up North Pass to the Bob's Big Boy on Riverside, to feed his still-drunk hangover with hash and eggs.

When Journeyman circled back an hour or so later, he found the suite door unlocked, but Todbaum's bedroom door shut, and no sign of Maddy. Instead, on the kitchen counter, he discovered a note in Todbaum's hand—*Go catch a flick, we could use a few hours*—atop two twenties. This was before cell phones. The desolate spaciousness between humans, between human moments, not yet filled in with chattering ghosts of reassurance. You could hear yourself not think. Journeyman saw a 10:50 matinee of *Raising Cain*, then ate a bulb-tanned hot dog and snuck down the corridor into *Unforgiven*. He wasn't woken until the credits rolled.

When he returned to the Starlet, the door was again unlocked. This time, Todbaum's door was open. Journeyman saw no signs, one way or another, of what activities might have taken place there. But Maddy's backpack was gone, all traces of her evaporated. And neither she nor Todbaum were to be found, the rest of that day, or into the night. Todbaum's car was gone too.

8.

THE CHAOS INSIDE THE QUIET

THE SHIVER AND CACKLE OF crows on an overhanging branch. The slick grinning madness within the man exiled to the Lake of Tiredness. The fever of life in an animal about to be slaughtered, only calmed for death. The sun, so placid through the trees, a fucking inferno exploding for eternity or until it fizzles. The stunned serenity of a vacated suite of rooms at the Starlet Apartments. The dystopia inside every utopia, the brain in every skull. The buzz and clatter of whatever it was that approached on the road today. The problem of me, thought Journeyman.

9.

THREE TOWNS

JOURNEYMAN LIVED IN TINDERWICK, THE peninsula's hub. The town functioned, before the Arrest, as the nerve center, where the ancient local families, the organic farmers, the off-the-grid types, the blue-blood summer people, the sailing folk, etc., all had been forced to mingle in détente before retiring to their mutual antipathies. Tinderwick housed the peninsula's library, along with other old institutions so dependent on fuel that they now comprised the local ruins: the gas station and car wash, the supermarket and post office, the firehouse (there had been an attempt to revive the firehouse on a horse-drawn basis, which flopped). The country club, its golf course now turned to cropland; a community radio station with a tall tower, much mourned; the restaurants and bars that had depended on tourism. Among such ruins, the bakery and the fish shack persisted on a barter basis, evoking a continuity with the town's more recent history. In other ways Tinderwick had reverted to a nineteenth-century form, when the town had been a wintry outpost stranded much of the year from the rest of civilization.

Yet even nineteenth-century Tinderwick would have featured a post office, regular newspapers from afar, and visitors landing by boat, things to inscribe the residents of Tinderwick as citizens of something wider. As Americans. New Englanders. Post-Arrest, any wider civilization remained unknown. There were just the two micro-cultures hemming them: the Cordon, which made their boundary from the larger mainland, and Esther's Landing, the isolated town at the peninsula's tip. The people of Esther's Landing could, by defi-nition, only bring outside news if it reached them by water. No such approach had been recorded, apart from the French boat. Since that had wrecked on Quarry Island, any news it might have conveyed perished with its crew.

The Cordon faced outward. Their folk did sometimes bring nerve-racking tales of organized assaults from precincts to the south and west, from New Hampshire. The Cordon's people were stoi-cal, flinty types; Eke was typical. Hardly storytellers. Shouldn't that make them trustworthy? Maybe, maybe not. The Cordon's accounts all underscored the need for their defensive measures, the hardening of a perimeter, the justifiability of their paranoiac vigilance. Mo-tive made all their tales suspect. Journeyman had wondered: how many hungry beggars equated to a berserker horde? Maybe just a half dozen.

The peninsula's second town, Granite Head, was where the old quarries were centered—those mysterious engines of the region's prospering for more than a century, before the appetite for gran-ite bank and skyscraper lobbies and bridge foundations in Boston and New York had been exhausted. The overgrown deep-bottomed quarry pits now not only functioned as natural freshwater fish hatcheries and swimming holes. Those of them with the right pro-portion and smoother walls made ice hockey rinks when the freeze was hard enough. Quarry hockey was a free entertainment relying on sturdy paraphernalia: metal skates, sticks, hard rubber pucks, and winter clothes.

Maddy lived in East Tinderwick, where the locavore and natural-growing community had centered itself, mid–twentieth century. The community blossomed in the 1940s, before hippies or foodies, though it paved the way for both. That was when the back-to-the-land gurus Seldon and Margot Stevedore bought several hundred acres of woods and overgrown farmland, to the wonder and consternation of the locals, and began parceling it out to young acolytes, so long as they were willing to bend their backs to the labor of growing food in a hostile terrain.

East Tinderwick was, therefore, the secret battery of the present survival of the community. The preservation and reinvention of the oldest methods, the mushrooming and berrying, the jarring and canning, the smoking of mackerel, the cellaring of root vegetables, had placed the community in a position to barter for their survival with the Cordon.

The Cordon had guns, when guns still worked. Once guns quit they had the authority of their willingness to do violence. They also had can openers, and Bush's maple-and-cured-bacon baked beans, only they were running out of the Bush's. The peninsula had farms that ran by horsepower even before the Arrest, simply because the trust-fund idealists and peak oil preppers and golden hippie grandchildren of the Stevedore sharecroppers thought it was a better and a nicer idea than lubing up and repairing a grimy old tractor. The peninsula had farmers who knew how to raise and murder a duck—as Journeyman had learned, ducks were *hard*—and a sausage maker who never wasted a drop of blood from a single murdered duck, if Journeyman could catch it and bring it to her. The peninsula had rose-hip-and-yellow-dock chutney, and smoked mackerel, and the best marijuana.

The Cordon liked these things, as well they should.

East Tinderwick was where Journeyman's sister had landed, after she fled Los Angeles, after the Starlet. East Tinderwick was where Maddy bought her own acreage, with a couple of partners from her senior-year off-campus house at Baginstock College, and, with them, founded the intentional community called Spodosol Ridge Farm. It was Spodosol where Journeyman had begun, after some time, visiting his sister during the summers, and it was where, over three decades later, he'd unintentionally found himself in residence at the Farm at the moment the Arrest occurred.

10.

MADELEINE

LONG BEFORE THE STARLET, JOURNEYMAN'S sister had struck him as dark. Not depressed, or gothy, more what's called saturnine. She seemed to occupy, helplessly, a square of Earth plagued by an excess of gravity, or shaded by a tiny storm cloud. Or both, gravity and cloud. It wasn't a thing she had the power to decorate or disguise, but a current that flew tangibly through her despite the adoption of any number of stances, attitudes, or enthusiasms—all the usual self-making of an adolescent person. Journeyman got to be the one who encouraged her by making fun of her. Or perhaps it was the reverse: that he made fun of her by his encouragement. Madeleine only stuck with things—field hockey, vegetarianism, certain tattooed and heavily pierced friends—that Journeyman had declared ridiculous, and unlikely to persist. She disappointed their parents freely, without giving them the satisfaction of seeing her fail. She only quit the violin on the day she'd finally achieved near sublimity, a celebrated recital after which she never lifted the bow again.

He'd never heard her volunteer an interest in music of any kind, let alone play it in her room.

On summer vacations at Rehoboth she steeled herself to swim

in the cold ocean, out a terrifying distance from the beach. She refused to be recruited for basketball but destroyed Journeyman in their backyard.

She possessed an uncanniness for problem-solving procedures, of a sort that caused her always to ace her math and science classes. Yet she eschewed abstractions and figuration both. She once explained to her brother how she visualized math problems: as a series of broken objects needing rearrangement into a more pleasing whole. Her hands moved while she solved them. She liked stuff.

One year she read all of Patrick O'Brian's Aubrey and Maturin novels, and shifted them from their father's shelves into her room. Yet she disliked the sailing cultures, the boaty folk, of coastal Delaware, of Fishers Island, and, later, of the peninsula to which she'd removed herself.

Journeyman never saw her take one drink at a high school party, but she'd accept a glass of wine from their father at dinner, the year before college. Journeyman didn't know if she'd been a drinker at college.

When Madeleine got her mathy hands into the soil, in college, and began to come home Christmases and Thanksgivings talking of loam and silt and hydrostasis, of cryptopores and mollisols, alfisols and spodosols, how could Journeyman have known she was describing her whole future concern, right down to the source of the name of the farm she and her fellow righteous oddballs would make their permanent home? Let alone that it would flourish and survive and become instrumental, a pin stuck through a tattered portion of reality when all the rest of it flew away?

11.

PERMANENT VACATION

THE FIRST TIME JOURNEYMAN VISITED Spodosol Ridge Farm he dropped in on his way back from a wedding on Mount Desert Island, a nuptial festivity that actually began with a chartered flight out of LAX into the Bar Harbor airfield. He'd at that point seen Maddy just once since the Starlet Apartments, on Fishers Island, at their father's seventieth birthday. Journeyman and his date to the wedding—a girlfriend who hadn't lasted long—had rented a car and meandered down the peninsula, the same road he walked today. On that day it had been smooth-paved, and made no particular impression on Journeyman apart from the length of it, and the depths of the woods that rose up intermittently like walls, the remoteness of the life his sister had chosen.

They stayed at the Farm less than two hours, Journeyman and his date. There was little he recalled of the visit, though he could place it in time: it was the year he'd written two episodes of a television show about a family living with a talking toaster, the first and, it would turn out, the last time Journeyman would earn a single-card credit on-screen for his writing. He did recall that Maddy and her six or seven homesteading companions at that time still bunked and cooked in one central lodge while laying foundations for the first of the individual homes on the Farm. He recalled being served a pasty, chunky yellow curried-vegetable rice in wooden bowls, and that his date didn't eat very much of hers.

That first visit, he and Maddy managed not to have a moment to themselves.

Three years later Journeyman visited the Farm in earnest. He was then at an early low ebb, the toaster show canceled and forgotten, his once-live pitches all gone dark, his manager not returning calls. Todbaum, on the other hand, was on the rise, through the ranks of the ordinary mortal assholes possessing a desk and a telephone, to assume what seemed his rightful place. He'd begun transforming himself into one of the town's sacred monsters, a packager known for wrangling talent and intellectual property into fertile conjunctions, for spooking money out of dim corners of the Pacific Rim and Eastern Europe. He was becoming one of those who defied the usual precept that, despite all the power talk, nobody really could make anything happen except for the seven or twelve bankable stars. Todbaum made things happen.

Journeyman's lack of work freed him to wander from L.A., though his money was growing thin.

If that second visit was a restorative one between Journeyman and his sister, it was a restoration to a cooled, firmer-edged place. She wasn't his kid sister any longer. He had to stop and apprehend who it was she'd become instead. Spodosol Ridge Farm thrived, five or six homesteads built, though several times a week the whole community still dined together in the central lodge. The fields were now joined by an elaborate greenhouse in which the Spodosolians produced miraculous Zone Five tomatoes, ripe in May and June. They'd allocated a quadrant of land to a group of migrant Mexican berry pickers, three families, who'd years earlier begun a roadside tamale stand from the blueberry fields, a hit with those who'd come here from afar and been starved for any authentic cuisine besides pie and lobster.

The tamale stand they'd subsidized into a real concern, a takeout business, now nestled inside Spodosol's weekly vegetable farm-drop enterprise, which had been embraced by the peninsula. Spodosol's produce had supplied restaurants in Tinderwick and Esther's Landing (East Tinderwick was too small for a restaurant, Granite Head too long in decline from its quarrying glory days), and also individual homes. If you weren't home, you'd leave a couple of twenties pinned on a counter in a kitchen left unlocked in exchange for a reusable wooden crate of what Spodosol Ridge pumped out of its fields.

Maddy had fallen in love with a woman. The obvious turn? Not to Journeyman. Astur Guutaale was Somali, a member of what Journeyman learned, to his surprise, was a substantial community centered in Lewiston. The two had met at the Common Ground Country Fair, a yearly gathering of agrarian hippies. Astur worked as a beekeeper. She'd traveled to the fair with a demonstration hive, and samples of honey, beeswax salves, and candles. Journeyman would come to know Astur well, later, in the permanent vacation that was to become his post-Arrest life. But not yet.

The sole mention of Todbaum came while Journeyman and his sister were swimming.

Maddy had had to lure Journeyman out. The ocean, whether at Rehoboth or Fishers Island or the monolithic blue fist of the Pacific, had never been Journeyman's thing. The cove here was sheltered, Maddy explained. The open surf broken by a dozen islands before it made its way to this inlet. The water warmed itself over the rocks, was nearly bathwater, or so she advertised. He went from the Farm with her that bright hot day and they immersed and floated out, two bobbing heads in salt froth. The cove wasn't only tolerably warm, it was filthy with green fronds, with dead jellyfish, with unidentified global-warming gloop, perhaps red tide or coliform. There were times Journeyman felt, accompanying Maddy through the natural world, that she'd filled his head with too much bioknowledge, that he couldn't quit being aware of everything teeming with rot and humidity, up to the food at the end of his fork.

Before Todbaum's name came up they discussed Journeyman's woes. His career drought, his romantic drought. They talked of their parents. Journeyman's mother's sense had begun to fail. At Christmas Eve dinner she'd cleared a half-full bowl of chowder from the table and drained it into an open silverware drawer. Their father's denial was absolute: he'd shut the chowder-filled drawer, and scowled Journeyman and Maddy to silence. What were they to do about it all? The Arrest would soon enough solve the conundrum for them, stranding them from news of whether their parents were even alive anymore. In this they were hardly alone.

Journeyman recalled the light twinkling on the ripples extending from their floating heads. The fronds and filth, the cool beneath the sun-warmed layer, the chrome-green horseflies that caused the siblings to slap at their heads and submerge. Maddy had seen Journeyman living at the Farm for five or six days; perhaps she'd begun to trust that he saw her for who she'd become. Might Journeyman be forgiven, that day? He craved more even than he'd already gained of Maddy's cool and acute compassion.

"I'm not working with Peter Todbaum anymore," Journeyman said. He'd weighted the emphasis in how he spoke the line, so it could be heard as a statement of policy rather than abject fact. Todbaum's ascent was fresh, and the two men were out of touch. Journeyman's bitterness toward Todbaum freed him to imagine he'd behaved valiantly on behalf of his sister in ways he hadn't.

"You really don't need to ever mention him again," said Maddy, not harshly, but with unmistakable firmness.

"Well, I figured—"

"Really not ever." She plunged her head below the water and stayed there awhile. There was no horsefly.

"Okay," he said when she surfaced.

So, it seemed to Journeyman later, Maddy had given him permission to leave unmentioned this fact: that he'd upon his return begun to work with Todbaum again. Indeed, Todbaum soon became the basis of Journeyman's whole livelihood.

12.

THE BLUE STREAK, PART 1

THE HORSES SNORTED. A CROW vamoosed. The supercar came around the corner and up the hill at once, gleaming in the sun and seeming to ripple off waves of heat-static around its perimeters, as though near and far at once. Eke waved Journeyman off the center of the road, onto the shoulder, to make way for it. The shiny abysmal engineered carcass. This was Journeyman's first impression: that a jet engine or hydrogen bomb had been mounted on a fantastic chassis, then been mated with an animal or insect. And then been turned at least partly inside out. The supercar was a monstrosity, a rupture to Journeyman's stabilizing premise, his self-situation. In its humming, seething, glistening actuality it made a blight in the very air. It seemed to destroy, or at least to collapse, time itself. This didn't strike Journeyman as a positive sensation. Following the Arrest, it had seemed that assaults on time—time's fragmentation, or insane velocity—had also been Arrested. Time had been allowed to recollect itself. To flow into bodies at an undistressed rate. The supercar wrenched a hole in those notions, which might now, it seemed to Journeyman, be exposed as sentimental. The supercar seemed to remember too well the pre-Arrest world, to drag fragments of smashed time in its wake.

Later, in the library, Journeyman found two pictures:

Journeyman X-Acto knifed these two images out of art books and added them to his file of recollections concerning the coming of Todbaum's supercar.

13.

YET ANOTHER WORLD, PART 1

WHEN TODBAUM BEGAN TO GENTLY orchestrate Journeyman's career, it was by bringing him in as a kind of triage expert on broken projects. Journeyman got script-polishing work—hugely remunerative and creatively pointless. His name wouldn't ever appear on-screen, but it did circulate in agents' offices, as he who'd salvaged such and such, always turned work in on time, never balked at a note. As a remora adopts a shark, Journeyman took work off Todbaum's leavings, and fed in his wake. Todbaum more and more loomed into a kind of living legend, reviled for his whims and abuses, for his savage truncations of personal visions, and yet a person whose calls one couldn't afford not to take. Journeyman's trace of legacy with him—you knew Todbaum at *school*? Sweet Jesus, what was he like *then*? Was he already . . . *Todbaum*?—became a minor point of fascination. It helped keep Journeyman's manager's phone ringing.

Between gigs Todbaum paid him a retainer, to tinker with a couple of Todbaum's slow-cooking pet projects, one or two of which Journeyman learned to care about. Journeyman found that if he sank enough hours into a given piece it gained a certain life. His fatal weakness, perhaps: he liked what he wrote. He liked draft one and he liked drafts seven and eleven too, and you could have wall-papered a multiplex with the editorial notes he received and mostly ignored. It was foolish to be offended at the suggestions the development and money people lavished on a draft. Nobody recalled what they'd said in the notes anyhow, not five minutes after they'd dictated them to their assistants.

Just one trace remained of Journeyman's and Todbaum's hard days' nights at the Starlet, that juvenile burst of activity, of treatments and pitches. That one trace was *Yet Another World*, the tale of alternate near-future Earths. One the cyber-dystopia, the other a wasteland of subsistence and looting, the eco-catastrophe Maddy had introduced into the conceit. For Todbaum, this was his gem, his secret unmade masterpiece. He paid Journeyman to write it, and to write it again. At one point Journeyman plopped out a 250-page version, a nearly unfilmable epic, which Todbaum personally dragged to Hertfordshire, England, there to batter down Stanley Kubrick's door with a personal appeal. Later, the project found a temporary home at DreamWorks, then Scott Free. Each time it collapsed, Todbaum hocked it out of turnaround from his own pocket, and set Journeyman to work again.

By the time of the Arrest, *Yet Another World* had evolved—stretched and sprawled—into a treatment for a wide-canvas premium cable series, the latest fashion. Its focus, more and more, on harbingers of eco-catastrophe, and collapsing borders, and the dawning of AI, and of virtual reality; the twenty-year-old story raced to keep up with the present. It would be the *Game of Thrones* of science fiction, Todbaum promised. First, he wanted it perfect, unassailable. He paid Journeyman to write all ten episodes of the first season, right to the unstoppable, heartbreaking cliff-hanger ending. Journeyman never thought to mention to his sister that the story to which she'd contributed such a crucial element was still alive, still nearly always open in a Final Draft window on his laptop. Or no—he thought of her participation frequently. He feared mentioning it to her, that was the truth.

When Peter Todbaum appeared in his supercar, the Blue Streak—its studded tires and tank treads almost entirely straddling the weed-riven, frost-heave-crumbled breadth of the road's old asphalt, its high-whirring engines and fans sounding nearly like a jet engine up close, escorted by Cordon cavalry horses and sputtering, barely functional shit-bikes—Todbaum's wonderful horrible Chitty Chitty Bang Bang colonized Journeyman's brain as a vision from the past's future. Or from the future of another past entirely. It was as though Todbaum's and Journeyman's long-unproduced masterpiece *Yet Another World* had at last been realized, not in the form of a feature film or television series but instead as a fact for which Journeyman might be liable. One world had broken through to another.

14.

THE BLUE STREAK, PART 2

"YOU'LL WANT TO STAND OVER here, Mr. Duplessis." Eke spoke precisely. Was it Journeyman's imagination, or had the scare quotes gone off "Mr." entirely? He'd gained in stature by being importantly connected to the supercar, even if he needed Eke's help to know the proper place to stand. "You hear him best from this vent."

Journeyman followed Eke along the crumbled shoulder, around the broad, complicated flank of the supercar, to find the vent in question: a flügelhorn-mouth at the front of the massive whining vehicle, protruding from amid a bank of square headlamps, and protected by a heavy grille. To follow Eke's lead was to stand directly before the car's nose cone, centered low between the mammoth front wheels, each the size of the rear tire of a giant tractor. At the mercy of the vehicle, should it suddenly move. This positioning of the speaker was unlikely, it seemed to Journeyman, to be accidental. Eke shrugged, expressing his rough sympathy at Journeyman's hesitation to place himself there.

The supercar steamed, wreathed in a cocktail of irreconcilable scents: butane, Kahlúa, coolant, melted copper wire. Journeyman felt sunburnt by its chrome dazzle, as though the reflected sun would etch hieroglyphic scribbles across his cheeks, his blinking eyelids. Here and there the metal carapace or the exterior piping was bruised, singed, scuffed, but that fact only seemed a further expression of the thing's fundamental indomitability.

Peter Todbaum's voice emanated, clear as a bell, unforgettable, and seeming to pick up at a place he'd left off some million revolutions of the galaxy ago. "Look at you, Sandy. The world's last innocent man, waltzing unharmed between the raindrops and these motorpsycho chuckleheads. How'd you pull it off?"

Journeyman looked up. A shadow-form bobbed, unreadable within a plexiglass globe cockpit. Could it be?

"Struck dumb to see me? Or did these lads maybe carve out your tongue for antipasto?" Todbaum's voice really was unchanged: fluent and abrasive, demanding love and capitulation.

"*Peter*?" said Journeyman.

"There you go. I came a long way to find you, Sandman. I drove all night for a year; I kept you in my thoughts every minute of the journey, too. You're a sight for sore eyes."

"How can it still drive?"

"A Passover miracle."

"I can't see your face."

"Hey, I'll get you up here for a soul kiss and look-around if you can tell the Rip Van Winkle Posse to slack off a little. These cowboys have been trying to climb up my ass for the past two days."

The loose-thronged Cordon people, whether mounted or dismounted from horses and bikes, didn't appear to be verging on an assault on Todbaum's supercar. Perhaps a residue of hostility had trailed the two parties up the coast, from early in their encounter. It might be the case that Todbaum couldn't read them from his cockpit. To Journeyman the Cordon men looked irritated, puzzled by the situation, perhaps eager to be shed of this problem.

"Eke?" Journeyman didn't know the names of the others. If Eke was not precisely the leader here, he might at least speak for the collective.

"Yeah?"

"My friend is asking whether you'd please take a few steps away from his vehicle."

"Thattaboy, Sandy. You've still got your ear for American lingo. Basically every two-bit Libertarian free-range asshole you'll ever meet is just waiting for someone to talk to them in Default Cop."

Eke grunted. He waved the horses back along the road. Journeyman couldn't know whether he'd overheard Todbaum's editorializing. Eke had an air of baffled deference. He might simply be language-hurt, after a long day's exposure to Todbaum's filibuster from the supercar's mouth hole.

Once Todbaum was satisfied by the slackening of the noose of Cordon men that ensnared him, he instructed Journeyman to move to what would have been the passenger side of an ordinary car. Journeyman heard a *pop*, as if a soda can had unsealed. Todbaum's bubble cockpit didn't raise. Instead, a large aperture dilated open, like a camera lens, just below the line of the cockpit. From out of the supercar's smooth-armored thorax, beneath where Journeyman stood, ladder-rung handholds slid out from beneath hidden panels. The ladder ascended to that weird open lens. Journeyman could climb, as if into a tree house. He did. He climbed into surely that most abhorrent of things, a mixed metaphor. For his name-seeking brain fell sick, the nearer it drew to the intoxicating machine. Was the supercar a camera, an insect, a jet plane, a tree house, a soda can? Since the Arrest, Journeyman tended to believe, things had only been themselves. The supercar was itself and everything else at once.

"Come right in." Todbaum spoke as if resplendent at the open door of his study, offering brandy or choice of cigars. Journeyman bent from the topmost rung, conscious of his own comic vulnerability to the men watching from below. He squirmed into the portal.

The fit was tight, but the passage was just a foot's thickness through the wall of the machine. He plopped onto the floor of the bright-lit capsule, at Todbaum's feet.

Journeyman smelled, he could swear, coffee.

Todbaum sat in a low bucket seat in front of the console that operated the car: blinking meters and sonar search screens, camera feeds showing the road and the horsemen and bikers in bug-lensed panorama, any number of mysterious bright-lit buttons and levers. Power. Electricity. Juice.

Using Time Averaging, Journeyman made the skinny, lined face into that of Peter Todbaum. The last time Journeyman had seen him, Todbaum had been fat. Like so many others, he'd gone on the Arrest diet.

Like no others anymore, he sat in a grotesque and intoxicating electrical machine, the power source of which was as yet unknown.

Like no one ever before on Earth, he was Todbaum. And so, seated high in his grotesque machine, steeping in the luxuriant absurdity of their reunion, and oblivious of the hostile men that surrounded his vehicle, Todbaum grinned at Journeyman and said, "I can read your mind, Sandman. You don't even have to speak."

"What am I thinking?" Journeyman replied, helplessly.

He pressed two fingers against one temple, miming ESP. "You want an espresso," he said. "You want it like nobody ever wanted a coffee before."

"You really have coffee?"

Todbaum showed Journeyman his demitasse. Empty, but with a fresh grime that made Journeyman's mouth instantly water. "Just a sec." He pushed it into a designated niche and pressed a button. A nozzle steamed and guttered. The cup filled. "Hope you don't mind sharing."

15.

THINGS TODBAUM TOLD JOURNEYMAN ABOUT THE BLUE STREAK

LATER JOURNEYMAN TOOK NOTES FOR his file, collecting things he heard Todbaum say that first day. Not all of them in the fifteen or twenty minutes that he spent nursing the espresso. Some Todbaum told him once they began moving down the road.

1. That, yes, Todbaum drove the thing from his home in Malibu. That he set out not quite a full year ago. Ten months.

2. That before embarking he'd survived the first three years of the Arrest without leaving Malibu. There, he and several others had for a time employed a private security force and survived as a kind of armed compound.

3. That nevertheless, through that time, he'd had the car already prepared, secretly waiting. "When every other fucking paranoid billionaire was sinking it all into private islands or safe houses or private islands with safe houses or underground Dr. Strangelove spider holes, I said to myself, why be a sitting duck? Who in God's name wants to sit around in *meetings*, with people you didn't even like when

they *had* money, deciding what to do the day the last sack of rice runs out?"

4. That, as he claimed to have predicted, the private mercenaries had in greed and desperation turned on the Malibu consortium. That only he had gotten out alive.

5. That the car could go almost seventy miles per hour on open highway, but that very little open highway was to be found between there and here anymore. That he'd had to go many times deep off-road, across fenced prairie and open desert and into forested mountain passes, all of which the car was equipped to traverse but at minimal speeds.

6. That at other times he'd sequestered in a simpatico community for a period of days or even weeks—in Boulder, Colorado; in Bloomington, Indiana; by a rural lake near Oberlin College in Ohio—and shared the benefits of the car with those who by dint of kindness he'd felt deserved it, but that invariably he'd grow rightly paranoid as plots began to encircle him, and so he'd hotfoot it out and on his way.

7. That he'd always, no matter the situation he'd discovered in his travels—and "hoo boy were there some stories" he'd tell— had Spodosol Ridge Farm in mind as an ultimate destination. That he'd known, somehow, that he'd find Journeyman and Madeleine intact there, "riding out the Arrest in style."

8. That it was called "the Blue Streak." That Todbaum had named it after a car in a story that his father used to tell him serially at bedtime. That the bedtime story was obviously extemporaneous—i.e., in Todbaum's phrase, a "bullshit shaggy-dog thing where he didn't have a fucking clue about where it was going, day to day."

9. That the Blue Streak was powered by a self-contained nuclear reactor. That it was retrofitted into the exoskeletal structure of a machine that had earlier been used to bore tunnels under the ocean. That it never needed fuel, and had not once needed repair. ("I wouldn't know the first thing about it. I'd probably just hit self-destruct and call it a wrap, game over, stick a fork in me.") That it was impossible to shut it off once it had been fired up. That Todbaum had been influential in the inception of the supercar project, suggesting it to its designer, based on a favorite film of his childhood called *Damnation Alley*. (Journeyman remembered he'd seen it, once Todbaum mentioned it. It starred George Peppard.) That its designer had built only three such machines before being kidnapped and never heard from again. ("Russia, gotta be.") That it cost Todbaum fourteen million dollars. That he didn't know who owned the other two.

10. That when he situated the machine in what he'd judged as a safe place, he could trigger a drill that sought groundwater to replenish his reserves. That before disengagement for travel it would by the same method bury his stored waste deep underground so that like prey it left no traceable spoor for anyone tracking. (Journeyman didn't point out that it sounded as though this meant he went everywhere contaminating potable aquifers that others might rely on.) The image of the Blue Streak planting its sucking tube where it landed made Journeyman see it, briefly, as a gigantic mosquito.

11. That his cockpit and sleeping cubicle were lead-lined, like a dentist's X-ray offices, to protect him from the risk of seeping radiation. (There was no mention of whether some radiated exhaust or contaminated expelled coolant posed a danger to those *outside* the vehicle.)

12. That the vacuum-sealed capsules of freeze-dried coffee stored deep in the Blue Streak's bowels actually had a gauge of their own on Todbaum's dashboard, and it showed that at the current rate he still had five months' worth of espresso. (He'd however polished off all the Macallan scotch before crossing the Susquehanna River.)

13. That the portal through which he'd admitted Journeyman was designed as a bladed trap, if necessary. It could cinch closed and murder someone who'd been lured up inside. Had Todbaum ever had to use it? "No, but I did crush a couple of jerks under the treads one night out around Santa Fe."

14. That the Blue Streak had endured numerous attacks. Those scuffed and singed places Journeyman had noted: each marked some assault, by medieval-style catapult or trebuchet, flaming arrow, or, before the guns had quit working, an Uzi or Glock. Todbaum indicated a place where a tracer bullet had lodged partway through the dual-layer safety glass of his windshield. The bullet was a perfect brass souvenir, its tip just through the glass to make a sharp little nipple. The glass was sealed tight around it, and uncracked.

15. That the only other person he'd admitted into his safe space, before Journeyman just now, was a woman he'd met in Pittsburgh who'd traveled with him as his companion as far as the outskirts of New York City, a locality into which Todbaum had refused to enter. She was looking for someone in Manhattan. She continued on foot. He, needless to say, had no idea what had become of her, but it wasn't likely to be good.

At some point in this initial telling, long after Journeyman had drained the tiny coffee, they found themselves interrupted. One of the Cordon men below—Eke, perhaps—began a loud rapping at the flügelhorn speaker, a sound that made its way up and drew their attention to the situation on the road. The rapping wasn't Morse code, but their message was clear. They wanted negotiations to resume.

16.

FOUNDER'S PARK

TODBAUM SHOWED JOURNEYMAN HOW HE opened the channel to listen and speak.

"You need our help, Mr. Duplessis?"

Todbaum grinned, and offered the microphone to Journeyman.

"Help?" said Journeyman.

"Just wanted to see if you're okay. Sounds like it." To Journeyman, Eke sounded stunned now, in the face of the supercar. Stunned or spooked, and seeking to tamp his anxieties down into the range of the normal.

Or it might be Journeyman who felt this way. "I'm fine," he said. "We're—old friends."

"Like the fellow said."

"Like he said, yes."

"Well, I guess if you want to consider him remanded into your custody or suchlike, me and these others will probably get going." *Remanded into custody?* Had Eke turned Default Cop back in the other direction now? The system of powers on this road felt unstable, perhaps booby-trapped. Was Journeyman meant to certify

Todbaum as his prisoner? If Journeyman refused, might he instead be considered Todbaum's co-captive?

Todbaum leaned in, shouldering Journeyman aside. "Gobble a plate of dicks, Harley-Davidson Man. I've never been in your custody for one minute and you know it. I guess you might be a custodian in the sense of the guy who swabs the halls and changes light bulbs at the junior high. That's obviously the kind of career you got cheated out of by the end of the world. The toilet attendant. Or *suchlike*."

"Mr. Duplessis?"

"Yes?" Journeyman said.

"Would you mind telling the other fellow that we're through talking with him for now?" Eke seemed to be restraining himself from harsher speech.

"Oh, sure."

"The elders just wanted me to be clear I'd passed him along to you. He's not to come back our way, least not unless some arrangement's made. If you don't want to climb down, I guess I can take your word that he hasn't got a gun to your head or—" Here Journeyman detected Eke restricting a final utterance: *suchlike*. Todbaum had gotten under Eke's skin, into his head. In this Eke stood in celebrated company. If only he knew.

"No," Journeyman said. "No gun to my head. So, you'll just go?"

"As I said at the start, there's interest in the operation of this car, Mr. Duplessis. At some point a contingent will want to come see what use could be made of it."

"Okay," said Journeyman. "Meanwhile we'll see your people at the usual time, then?" Journeyman meant for the food drops, the ordinary tribute.

"Imagine so."

"We're always glad to see you, Eke."

"Good day now, Mr. Duplessis."

At that, the Cordon horses and the two motorcycles unsurrounded the Blue Streak and retreated up the road. Todbaum and

Journeyman watched. Journeyman noted again the puzzle of their bandages, their recent injuries: had Todbaum, and his Blue Streak, inflicted these? At a certain distance the Cordon men stopped and turned. Perhaps they wished to see the supercar begin to progress deeper into Journeyman's territory, and farther from theirs. Then they were gone from sight. Todbaum was Journeyman's problem now.

What should Journeyman propose? The only answer was to pilot south into Tinderwick. There were no other directions. A mad impulse seized Journeyman then, to turn Todbaum right, onto the road to the Lake of Tiredness. Could he hide him there, with Jerome Kormentz? Persuade him this was the entirety of the survivor's community? What would they make of one another? But this was idiotic. Todbaum knew of the towns, of Maddy's farm. He'd had confirmation from the Cordon.

Now Todbaum set out, in any event. The whirring and seething of the machine was accompanied again by the grinding sound of the treads, that grim hum Journeyman had detected when the thing was still out of sight. Over his shoulder, too, Journeyman saw that it had a mapping capacity. Journeyman hadn't seen a working GPS since the Arrest. Did satellites still orbit the Earth? Anyone with a good telescope could know, but if Journeyman knew anyone with a good telescope, he wasn't aware of it.

The line representing the road to Tinderwick throbbed blue as the supercar's transit resumed. Journeyman was a mere passenger. Yet, no matter Todbaum's expectation, Journeyman wouldn't be party to bringing Todbaum's Blue Streak to Spodosol Ridge Farm, to implant its feeding and pooping tubes in his sister's precious soil. Todbaum's map already indicated the turn, east off Main, toward East Tinderwick.

So Journeyman formed his intention: to steer Todbaum and his craft toward a mooring by the water, near the boat landing behind the old post office, at the center of the smaller town, on the acre of land they called Founder's Park.

17.

ISLAND AND LIGHTHOUSE

THE BLUE STREAK RUMBLED INTO Tinderwick, carrying Todbaum and Journeyman. The settlements on the road thickened, as they passed Brenda's Folly Farm and Proscenium Farm, until suddenly revealing the high street of the old village—the Presbyterian church, the bookstore, the music conservatory. Tinderwick was tumbleweed-quiet at midday. Farmers in their fields. Tinkerers and canners in their barns or summer kitchens. Children up at the old school. Journeyman felt sealed in doom, atop the Blue Streak. Unable to hear the crows or bees, the blue-spangled canopy of trees mediated by the cockpit's bubble, revealing not a whisper of wind. They hit Main Street. Todbaum piloted leftward, toward East Tinderwick, without any help from Journeyman. Soon, past the old cemetery, the Civil War monument, they'd returned to forested road, the supercar brushing silently through branch tops. No one had tried to halt them in town. No one had seen them at all.

So, they ground on, in the direction of Spodosol.

It was as though Journeyman had been sucked up not into Todbaum's car but into his old friend and employer's devilish brain. Or not sucked up. Journeyman had ascended voluntarily. Stepped off his frost-heaved asphalt, out of that routine which now seemed miraculous for its calm, and squeezed through Todbaum's murderous porthole, to accept a nuclear-fueled espresso and to hitch a ride aboard this ticking bomb. They moved toward East Tinderwick. Journeyman needed to execute his thin plan, his stalling maneuver.

"When did you last see the ocean?" Journeyman asked.

"Good question!" said Todbaum. Was he mocking? "Not since I blew town."

Journeyman plowed on. "So, I'm thinking of where you ought to, uh, put down stakes to begin with. There's a good spot for this . . . thing of yours . . . by the water. Sort of the town commons. Nobody will feel you're sneaking up on them."

"Ocean view? Sounds deluxe."

"Well, water view, I should specify. There's an island between our harbor and the ocean."

Founder's Park looked onto a narrow strip of land called Quarry Island. The uninhabited island's length blocked any view of the open horizon. A hundred and two hundred years earlier its bedrock had been heavily worked, produced blocks of raw granite shipped on barges, to be polished and fitted into the lobbies of big-city municipal buildings. At the peak of the work dozens of men overnighted there. Their collapsed shacks were a desolate remnant, hemmed by new-growth trees. One titanic hunk of quarried granite stood like a windowless building on the island's south edge, atop its ocean-facing cliffs. Whether abandoned because of some internal flaw or left as a monument, no one knew.

Journeyman heard himself babbling out bits and pieces, as if trying to keep Todbaum entertained during a pitch. ". . . some people say the island's stone even went into the pilings for the Brooklyn Bridge—"

"Of course it did. It's perfect, Sandman. I'll sleep to the lapping of the waves, knowing I and I alone crossed from sea to shining fucking sea."

Journeyman thought of the French boat, a mystery Todbaum would appreciate.

It had crashed on Quarry Island the winter before, on a night when fog obscured the moon and the island and coast were crusted in a new snow. The French crew had likely failed to distinguish Quarry Island from the more distant mainland; between lay coastal shelf, slimy barnacle-covered granite that made low tide a peril for the most local sailors even in daylight. Their boat ran three sails. If the two men found dead had been the sole occupants for an ocean journey from Europe, they'd had their hands full. The boat was shattered, the men drowned, or frozen before they could drown. There'd been no chance to ask what form the Arrest had taken in France.

Journeyman told Todbaum how the boat had been torn across the hacksaw barnacles by the action of the tides. The bodies too. Journeyman had been part of the cleanup crew. Not utterly unlike his work for Augustus the butcher.

"Saved your people offing those frogs, I guess!"

Offing them? Journeyman was nearly embarrassed to say that the three towns hadn't killed anyone since the Arrest, not that he was aware of. He'd disappoint Todbaum's appetite for Armageddon. "We didn't find any weapons . . . We can't know what they were thinking, of course . . ."

"I'm kidding, Sandman! You're good people! You leave that unsavory shit to the Cordon folks, don't you?"

"We've never asked the Cordon to kill anyone."

"They'd have cracked me open like a bone and sucked the marrow if they'd figured how."

Perhaps if you'd treated them as more than skunks or porcupines on the road—but this, Journeyman didn't say. Todbaum might be right. Who knew what he'd endured? There was that windshield bullet. Journeyman would hardly be the only one eager to hear Todbaum's account of his journey. The towns had argued for weeks whether the French sailors had fled danger or brought news of a distant reorganization.

It was then that the towns had begun talk of constructing a lighthouse on Quarry Island. A tower, at least, with a standing flare, to ignite on nights like that which had lured the French boat to ruin in their death-trap harbor.

"Some of us have a theory that there'll be another French boat," Journeyman told Todbaum now. "The chance to know what it's like over there, over the ocean . . . it's tantalizing, don't you think?"

"Oh, there'll be another French boat. The French always do things in threes, isn't that the formula?"

Journeyman didn't know that formula. "There's been talk of a lighthouse, if we could find a way . . ."

By now the supercar had cruised through the village center of East Tinderwick—the old Grange Hall, the post office, the boat-yard. The town center was tiny, and still. The vibrant part of East Tinderwick, thanks to the homesteading followers of Seldon and Margot Stevedore, was out at the end of long dirt roads, on the organic farms. Journeyman wouldn't lead Todbaum to any of those, let alone Spodosol. He pointed him leftward, past the P.O., into Founder's Park.

"A lighthouse!" Todbaum seemed delighted. "You people are ingenious. Fueled by human waste, huh?"

"My sister's on the committee." Journeyman winced. He hadn't meant to mention Maddy. "We'd have to figure out some kind of way to keep a bonfire lit, on top—"

"We should make it look like the Statue of Liberty! Only crooked, like at the end of *Planet of the Apes*."

"Ha." Now the Blue Streak lurched toward the water, toward the park, and Quarry Island. There, Todbaum stopped it. To their left, the small park's scrappy play structures: an old swing set and slide, a tire swing too, and a bare basketball hoop presiding over a quadrant of concrete. Founder's Park wasn't mowed anymore. The grass was high and yellow. Journeyman yearned for more cover, but there wasn't any. The supercar was a sore thumb, unless he could persuade Todbaum to keep driving and sink it into the muck of the harbor.

"Seriously, that's hot shit, Sandman. There's a lot of raw potential up here."

"Potential? Uh, yes . . ." *Potential for what?* Journeyman wished to scream.

Had Todbaum, master producer, come here to make some spectacle?

Was he location scouting?

18.

BEFORE JOURNEYMAN LEFT HIM, TODBAUM GREW SENTIMENTAL

JOURNEYMAN EXPLAINED THAT HE HAD to go and leave Todbaum there. Would Todbaum be okay? Did he need anything in particular? Journeyman encouraged Todbaum to feel free to exit his machine and stretch his legs, to walk in Founder's Park or even stroll through town. Todbaum laughed. "I've been living in this thing for nearly a year, Sandman." Journeyman told him no one would try to hurt him here, in East Tinderwick, and he laughed again. "I won't hurt them either." Then, before Journeyman could try to exit the machine, Todbaum grew abruptly sentimental. He halted Journeyman by placing his hands on Journeyman's shoulders.

"You ever think why?"

"Why what?"

"Why this? Why fucking *this*? Let me put it another way. Where does a person go? To a book? What do you reach for, Sandman: Philosophy? Psychedelics? Dostoyevsky? I mean in the Hour of the Wolf, at the end of the day, whatever. Is there some guru you like, under a tree? By a lake?" Journeyman was briefly perplexed: could Todbaum actually be making reference to Jerome Kormentz? Todbaum stared into Journeyman's eyes, then twisted his mouth and made a sound: *"Phhaaaghhh."* The sound was familiar: Todbaum's oral-flatulent dismissal of all received wisdom. Previously, it would have been that wisdom dictating typical action in his chosen sphere, the industry.

"I think I did this," he said.

"What?"

"I think my hatred did this. I hated it all that much, Sandy. What I'd become. Those Malibu fucks with their private islands, their secret escape hatches. Worst people in the world. I was one of them, even if I was a thousand times smarter and bigger."

Ah, yes. This had nothing to do with Kormentz. Todbaum had no idea Kormentz existed.

"So, give it up, Sandy, where do you look?"

"When I look at the Arrest?"

"Sure."

"I don't know. Maybe the natural world has a kind of imperative that we can't know. That even if we're part of it, we're just one part." Journeyman was surprised he'd located the words. They were stopgap, cobbled from beliefs he'd gathered others nearby might hold.

"Huh, some kind of animist shit? Nice try, I'll give you that. For me, it's consciousness. The only puzzle they never solved. My own consciousness, specifically. I'm not afraid to root around in the sub-basement. When I say bigger than those Malibu fucks, I mean unimaginably bigger, like a tesseract—bigger on the inside than on the outside. When I delve in there I see a *lot* of correspondences."

"Correspondences . . . between?"

"What's the story I couldn't quit puzzling over? *Yet Another World.* Now look."

"You think we're living in your pitch?"

"It all came out of my head. Except one part."

In this craziness, Journeyman nevertheless knew not to imagine that Todbaum meant the thousands of draft pages he, Journeyman, had elucidated from what had come out of Todbaum's head. "What part is that?"

"Madeleine's. You remember."

Journeyman did. He said nothing.

"That's where we are. I mean, open your eyes, Sandman."

"In my sister's head?"

"In some combination of the two. That's the point. Me and her. Not one or the other."

"You and Maddy made the world?"

"We were living in mine, now we're living in hers. We went through the lens. You know what I'm out here chasing, Sandman?" There were tears in Todbaum's eyes.

"What?"

"Something sustainable." From the pilot of the nuclear-fueled, espresso-making guillotine the word was obscene. "We're going to solve this together, I can feel it. Bring the halves together again."

Todbaum believing he'd seen the Arrest coming; this was only typical. He'd made billions betting on a hunch about the culture's appetite for tentpole movies about giant robots from outer space. He now claimed to have the only functioning supercar—he was the only Todbaum. Why not believe he could do better than live at the Arrest's mercy? Journeyman felt the nightmare logic land in him, like the hook of an old song. Todbaum wanted to break the Arrest open, put his signature on it. *To piss inside the tent*, to use his own language.

Todbaum pulled Journeyman into an embrace. Here at last was the thing the supercar had been designed to cradle and nourish, to usher eastward—the yolk in the eggshell. Journeyman felt Todbaum's thin shoulders. Todbaum's dumb unrepentant belly, pressed against his own. Todbaum had been thin and slack in college, a walking question mark. Then fat and hale in his ascendancy, years through which he retained a trainer, cook, and masseuse, when he'd entertained every appetite and habit in the book, when each night had been devoted to self-murder and each morning to reanimation of the corpse. Now, eggplant-shaped, he sagged into Journeyman's arms like an overripe one. No beneficiary of post-Arrest physical labor—captive in his supercar, what had he done besides push buttons?—he'd nevertheless shed weight, like everyone.

They parted on the basis by which life was lived now: Journeyman would return with something good to eat. A promise he could keep. Todbaum dilated the portal, and Journeyman was released to climb the supercar's external ladder.

Exiting the park, Journeyman spooked a string of wild turkeys bobbing through the reeds. Unlikely birds, Darwinian jokes, ready food. They'd thrived lately, population exploding thanks to a climate-based shift in the fates of their predators. Journeyman didn't pause to cede them the road, as he'd ordinarily have done. They bolted into the sun-soft woods.

Why had Journeyman allowed Eke to place Todbaum in his hands? Why couldn't they have just murdered him?

The Blue Streak was too strong or they'd have done it.

He had to protect his sister, her farm, the present state of reality, all.

He, Journeyman, the town joke, the conveyor of packages, the emissary.

The day, the town, the road, all was as Journeyman left it— peaceable, pensive, continuous. Arrested. So long as he didn't turn his head to see what lay behind: the Blue Streak's occupation of the town commons. As he crossed the ruined paving where the turkeys had thronged, toward the shrouded path to Spodosol Ridge Farm, there to deliver some rendition of his crazy news of the Blue Streak's arrival, Journeyman mourned his present world, with that deep chest ache certifying a-thing-already-lost.

19.

THE STARLET APARTMENTS, PART 2

DID JOURNEYMAN CALL THE POLICE? ("Two recent college graduates slipped off in one another's company. I'm worried the attraction may not be mutual.") He did not. Did he call his and Maddy's parents? ("The thing is, Dad, my friend is a—") Well, what was Todbaum?

Journeyman didn't have to decide. No, he conducted his own search, first on foot, then, humiliatingly, by taxicab. He hit the bars, the widest circuit, the Dresden, the Viper Room, Musso & Frank, places he and Todbaum had visited and others they'd intended to. He invaded the Chateau Marmont. Journeyman pictured his sister and his friend on a revel, in other words. As though Todbaum had simply nudged Journeyman aside and plugged Maddy into his place—maybe they were trying to pick up women *together*. Although it wasn't the likeliest picture in the world, it was the best Journeyman could conjure up.

He had to direct the last cab back to a cash machine near the Starlet just to pay off the meter. His account was below five hundred dollars. He walked to Bob's Big Boy again, the second time this day, one which had turned to night, his first night in Los Angeles not in the company of Todbaum. Had something happened to his friend and his sister? The question was whether something had happened to Maddy. When Journeyman walked back, he checked what had become Todbaum's usual parking spot. The BMW was returned.

He ran up to find them. The suite was still empty, as he'd left it. Journeyman's sense of helplessness, instilled by hours at the mercy of Los Angeles without a vehicle, was now a self-fulfilling thing. He'd been taught the name for this in college: *learned helplessness.* Todbaum's BMW seemed to move of its own accord. Meanwhile the suite doors locked and unlocked themselves, the humans refusing to appear. He stared at the empty rooms in dumb wonder, as if contemplating an M. C. Escher drawing.

When sleep began to insist itself, Journeyman stretched out on the couch, where Maddy had camped. This wasn't in solidarity, exactly. More that a retreat to his room might invite further shenanigans at his expense. He wanted to stake out the entrance. Perhaps he should drag a pillow and blanket down to the street and sleep across the hood of the BMW so it couldn't be started again without his knowledge, but no. That was the onset of the crazy thinking. No one interrupted his sleep, and he didn't wake until late the next morning.

The riddle's answer was there in Journeyman's mind when he woke. So simple: the Starlet Apartments had plenty of vacancies. Todbaum's trick was perfectly in character. It fit his complacency, his stated preference for use of "available materials," also his way of throwing money at any situation. Journeyman had slept in his clothes, and had only to tie his sneakers to rush outside. The complex was structured so that from the pool area he'd gain a view of both levels. Maybe he could judge, even in daylight, which formerly vacant suite showed signs of new occupancy.

The day's party was underway. Or the previous night's had never ended. Party such as it was. A pair of women in midriff-knotted T-shirts and bikini bottoms sat on the kiddie steps, immersed to the waist, smoking American Spirits, with melting ice cubes in a tumbler for an ashtray. One of these was Journeyman's might-have-been-couldn't-remember.

"Where's your suit?"

"Have you seen Peter or Maddy?"

"They're busy little rabbits."

"What does that mean?"

"No time for you or me, baby. They're in the twilight zone." Then she noticed Journeyman casting his eyes along the balcony, reading curtains left to right. "Something wrong?"

"I need to talk to them."

"Well, go talk to them, then." Her glance was enough, just. Journeyman followed it to the right door.

It was locked, the curtain drawn. Journeyman wasn't going away. He made conspicuous noise with the door handle, and tapped at the window too. When the door cracked open—he heard the chain come off first—Todbaum stuck his head out.

"Just in time," Todbaum said. "We're out of ice and a few other things—" Though Todbaum wore the same Indonesian silk robe in which he'd paced all day around the suite below, dictating while Journeyman worked the Typestar's keyboard, his wallet was in his hand. He peeled out a series of twenties and began to stuff them through the gap. "I'll find you the car keys, just a minute—"

"I want to talk to Maddy."

"Not just now, Sandman."

"I'm serious, Peter."

"Awww, don't make me spell it out in plain English, you're breaking my heart. The reason we're talking like this is Maddy asked me to make you go away."

"Let her tell me that." A line Journeyman would have scratched from a draft. Should he reach through the door's gap and grab Todbaum by the collar now? He didn't.

Todbaum lowered his voice. "We're all consensual adults around here, Galahad. Don't infantilize your sibling."

"Are you . . . working on the treatment? *Yet Another World?*"
Journeyman heard himself. Was he really so daft?

"Maddy hasn't said one word about it. Not since making her
sublime intervention. I don't even think she's interested."

"Well then, what are you doing?"

"What do you think we're doing? Took the edge off, basically.
Got my ashes hauled. Which, if I'm judging right, is what you're in
need of and didn't get. Am I correct, sir? You find yourself passed
over by the poolside?"

"Let me talk to her."

"No tears were shed, no coltish animals were harmed in the
making of this major motion picture."

They haggled. Journeyman's appeals drew only scorn from Todbaum, who'd stepped outside, now, to stand with Journeyman on
the balcony. Then, just as they gained the attention of the women
at the pool, below, they were both halted—by the *click* of the lock
behind Todbaum.

20.

HIS LAST FLIGHT

VISITING MADDY, JOURNEYMAN ALWAYS WENT LAX to Boston on the red-eye, then a morning hop to Bangor. The last time, the June before the Arrest, he did this also. Was the carrier JetBlue? How could it matter to remember? The point about his last flight was that it was that great rarity anymore, the flight not overbooked. Or maybe less a rarity, in the time just before the Arrest, when many things were changed and jumbled up in unaccountable ways. They discussed this frequently those first weeks at Spodosol: had there been warning signs? Yes. There'd been a decade's or a century's worth of warning signs. But had there been indicators on the close horizon, a prodrome of the Arrest? Probably that too.

Yet to enter a plane and find even a scattering of empty seats, still a novelty.

This red-eye was half-full. Maybe less—many had a row to themselves. Journeyman did. A throwback. The atmosphere was giddy, the attendants blithe. The passengers changed seats, slept without seat belts. A kid ran paces up and down the central aisle. Journeyman refilled his own coffee in the back of the plane and was rewarded with a mere knowing smile.

Yet when they landed it was to be informed they weren't approaching the ordinary gates in Boston, and that those with connecting flights might wish to seek alternate plans. The plane was moved into a special quarantine area, there to sit for a long while, all aboard growing restive, before it was even unsealed. A kind of shock came over the passengers, all defiance evaporating, when those who'd come to meet the plane wore hazmat suits.

Journeyman never learned what they were looking for or whether they found it, or whether some panic was left in his wake when he departed the airport.

There was no longer a connection to Bangor. Journeyman Lyfted to a bus station, there hopped a Concord Lines bus, a seven-hour journey through tedium, pulling in at every town along Route 1. He called Maddy and she drove down to pick him up in Belfast. She brought Astur, too. They were a public couple now. Had Astur had to shake off her community's prohibition on lesbianism? Or hadn't there been one? There certainly wasn't in Belfast, Maine. They'd had a late lunch at a restaurant, a lovely one, called Chase's Daily.

Airplane, cell phone, automobile, restaurant.

All things now gone.

The Arrest, in full, came six weeks later.

21.

ASTUR

IT WAS THE SPECIAL SENSATION of moving through time that had recalled Journeyman's last flight. Todbaum's supercar had induced it. Like the flight, the Blue Streak had crossed west to east. And the controls themselves, inside Todbaum's cockpit, seemed to mangle different centuries together, realms of before and after science.

He ran into Astur first, as he moved down the Spodosol road carrying his Telluride backpack and the burden of his impossible fact. His sister's lover startled him as she approached. She appeared from behind a concealing wall of ripening, silk-humid corn, a wall whose fingerlike leaves barely rippled in the summery air. Astur wasn't as tall as Maddy, but she was tall. Journeyman's height.

"Good day, Sandy."

"Astur! I was just looking for you guys!"

"We hadn't expected you until dinner tonight. I hope you're still coming?"

"Oh, sure—" Tuesdays were a regular dinner for Journeyman, at the general open-table gathering at Spodosol. It returned to him, then, that today was a Tuesday. Still an ordinary Tuesday for anyone who hadn't seen the supercar. "I was just—I'll walk home, and come with my bicycle tonight—" Journeyman usually bicycled between the towns after dark.

"Or we can loan you one of the Farm's bicycles," said Astur. "If you'd like to stay the afternoon."

"No, I don't mind walking back, I just—something came up." He'd been whisked here so easefully in the Blue Streak's cockpit. Time and space, distance on a road, these were not what they had been before Todbaum's arrival. Further, Journeyman had been converted instantaneously into a fumbling liar, and Todbaum's accomplice. "Any idea where I can find Maddy?" he asked.

"Yes, the Grange Hall," Astur spoke as if reminding him of something he ought to have known. Journeyman often couldn't tell when she was joking. It demolished his confidence in trying to read her. Journeyman knew he was easy to read.

"Oh?"

"The village association's afternoon meeting. Theodore Nowlin's proposal." She offered a brief eye roll, inviting Journeyman's enjoyment.

"Of course." Nowlin, a great bearded slab of a man, a widower in his seventies, had returned to the peninsula to retire to his family's East Tinderwick farmstead, on which he cultivated a large flower bed along with his vegetables. This, after several decades' employment as an arc welder at the Bath Iron Works, constructing navy destroyers. Nowlin's five-generations-in-Maine claim, his salty street cred, was a thing Journeyman found irksome.

Nowlin's proposal was for an ocean expedition. His stated belief, that the Cordon was made of inlanders and lacked in oceangoing expertise. They showed no capacity for patrolling the coastline. Nowlin argued that a vessel of good size could ride out far enough to circumnavigate the Cordon's vigilance, to make contact with the fine folk he imagined still ran the show in Bath and Brunswick. Nowlin had been trying for months to divert East Tinderwick's engineering resources away from the lighthouse tower on Quarry Island, in favor of his big boat plan. No one quite had the heart to point out the swarm of unknowns upon which his dream depended.

"Is something the matter, Sandy?"

"No, I'll just wait up at the Farm, I guess." Journeyman lacked a clear intention. But rushing to the Grange Hall to find Maddy in the company of so many responsible East Tinderwickians wasn't appealing. He'd either have to divulge his insane news to them collectively, or actively seek to deceive them. He wanted to whisper it to Maddy. As if it were merely a whisper.

"Your work is done?"

"Yes," Journeyman said. "All I did was visit the Lake of Tiredness." A lie of omission. But Astur had asked about work. Not whether he'd bummed any rides.

Astur raised an eyebrow. "Ah." Journeyman's visits to Kormentz were a surefire conversation killer. "Well, then, why don't you come out with me on the water? The wind is perfect today."

"Oh! That's where you're going?"

"I'd love your company."

"In a *boat*, you mean?" Astur had left Somalia at nineteen, with her family, by boat. Despite that terrifying passage—or because of it?—she liked sailboats, and the sea, and frequently went out solo in a shellback. She'd ferried Journeyman and other nonsailors to Quarry Island the week of the cleanup of the bodies and wreckage from the French boat. Astur was able to row a peapod from the shore to a moored sailboat like a champion, better than Journeyman could imagine ever being able.

"Why not, Sandy?" Astur's smile was incredibly warm. "Everyone else is at the meeting. My own work was completed this morning. Are you needed elsewhere?"

"Um—"

"You seem heavy."

"I do?" Journeyman felt not heavy, but weightless, detached, invisible. Or wished he were invisible. He saw the problem with his plan to merely dawdle at the Farm, waiting for Maddy to return: if Astur wasn't diverted from her course, she'd spot the Blue Streak from the water herself. He felt increasing panic: there wasn't any way he could prohibit or prevent this. Who knew what Todbaum might be doing now, and to whom?

"Why aren't *you* at the meeting?" Journeyman asked her. "The lighthouse project is as much yours as anyone's."

"Exactly. My presence isn't required, since my views are well represented. Theodore Nowlin doesn't see me as a person separate from Madeleine, really." Journeyman understood her to mean Nowlin didn't see her as a person, period. He wouldn't presume to articulate this.

"You're a vote," Journeyman said. "C'mon, I'll go with you, we've got him surrounded."

"Our votes aren't needed, Sandy. It's decided by consensus, as you'd know if you ever attended one of our meetings."

"Well, I live in Tinderwick." He felt accused of something, everything.

"So, why concern yourself? Come with me instead."

"On the boat?"

"Yes, Sandy, on the boat! Why should that be so ridiculous to you? This day won't come again. Whatever's worrying you, it can wait."

He was tempted. Though perhaps because he felt tempted to abstraction, dissociation, to absenting. Why not enter a small boat with his sister's girlfriend, to consider the whole thing from the beneficent waters? There it would be, the coastline, with its little traces of their town poking through the dense tree line: the boat put-in, the playground equipment, Todbaum's silly car—all to be beheld, all to be . . . well, what? Beheld. That might be enough.

But one thing *wasn't* possible—to sail from the coastline of himself. Journeyman didn't, for instance, like boats. He couldn't experience any pleasure aboard them. Did Astur know this already, and was therefore needling him, or was her consideration sincere, in which case he'd have to disappoint her? But this was idiotic—of course it was sincere. Todbaum had only reentered Journeyman's life an hour earlier, and already Journeyman projected the other man's interpersonal Machiavellianism in every direction.

"I'll walk with you as far as the put-in," Journeyman said. "There's something there I have to show you."

"Okay, I'll enjoy your company on the walk. Maybe at the put-in you'll change your mind."

"Maybe I will."

"I have two life jackets."

Sure, he thought but didn't say, but have you got a built-in espresso machine?

22.

THE STARLET APARTMENTS, PART 3

IT WAS LIKE COMEDY, ONLY not funny. Todbaum stood in his robe, locked out. He appealed, in turn, to the closed door, to Journeyman, to the onlookers, to the nowhere-to-be-found apartment manager. The pool women involved themselves, displaying a remarkable capacity to seem drunker in a crisis, despite not drinking, as if drawing on unseen reserves. Their semi-boyfriends appeared before long, too. They hustled Todbaum away to be placated or reasoned with. The women wanted to speak to Maddy through the door, to tell her that Todbaum wasn't near, that it was safe to open up. Todbaum reappeared and demanded his car keys. The process of placation had to begin anew. Journeyman was given the car keys instead. Maddy would be smuggled downstairs—she'd refused to speak with her brother while on the premises, but he'd be allowed to drive her to LAX. Journeyman should wait in the car. He supposed he was being managed too, though he didn't recall any unreasonable behavior on his part, or any reasonable behavior, either—he felt he'd stood dumbly to one side, a helpless observer. Were the absurd strictures Maddy's own, or conjured by these loopy intermediaries? Soon enough Maddy appeared at the car, fully dressed, bearing the overstuffed hiker's pack, which she shoved into the back seat. She wore a turtleneck, far too hot for the occasion. Was it this that made her cheeks look so red? It reminded Journeyman of how she'd dressed as a teenager, to conceal the flaky skin of her neck.

"Go."

Journeyman protested. Maddy made it clear that he should drive, if he wanted even a syllable back. He drove.

"Where to?"

"The airport."

"Wow," he said. "You have a ticket?"

"They sell tickets."

"So, I'm your cabdriver? After you vanish for two days?"

"*Did* I? Vanish? Is that what I did?"

"I don't know, Maddy. Maybe that's not the word for it. Are you going to tell me what happened in there?"

Journeyman felt her emphatically not-looking at him as he slid Todbaum's car onto the 101. "I am not going to tell you what happened in there." These words stacked like bricks between him and his sister.

"Okay, fine, whatever. So, you're just going to let Peter completely ruin this whole thing for you? I was going to show you L.A." The car was hot. He cranked the AC. For once there was no traffic.

"Well, you didn't show me L.A. You showed me, what is this? Burbank? Toluca Lake? You showed me the Starlet Apartments. But maybe you don't know the difference."

"You sound—" Journeyman started this despite himself, and finished it that way too. "You sound like Peter." A part of him wanted to wreck Todbaum's car, to wreck the squalid progress of this event. He and his sister would walk back, as he'd walked between destinations, searching for her.

"That would be natural, since I've been listening to nothing else for days."

The heat in the car was the heat of Maddy's face, the bottling of unwept tears while she razed the hillside with her eyes.

"You didn't have to listen for days," he said. "I didn't ask you to do that."

"No, Sandy, you didn't ask me."

Journeyman couldn't compute her sarcasm. "Why didn't you just walk out of the room? He didn't restrain you in some way?" Journeyman suspected Todbaum's predilections.

"Not in any way you wouldn't recognize."

Journeyman reached over and tugged at her turtleneck's collar. The imprints of Todbaum's teeth were just below, red dents, already purplish-edged. Her skin was otherwise smooth, no sign of psoriasis. She slapped away his hand.

"Before you say anything, Sandy—"

"What?" He should have been enraged. He felt baffled.

"That isn't the matter; it isn't anything."

"You like that?"

"I like that." She was angry now. Journeyman would always stand, he saw, at the doorway of those with predilections, those like Todbaum and his sister shared, and feel a fool for wondering. For not belonging even at the doorway.

"So, what's the matter?" he said sulkily, unwilling yet to be contrite.

"Maybe you can have a thing you like, but have it in the wrong way."

"You weren't his captive? He didn't stop you from leaving?"

"He did stop me, but not how you think."

"How?"

"With words."

"What kind of words?"

"Pull over."

"What?"

"I'll find a real cab. Or I'll hitchhike, that ought to go well. I don't want to be in this car anymore, Sandy."

"Let me drive you where you want to go. To the airport. Do you even know what airline?"

"Domestic whatever."

"Domestic whatever, right."

They sat in silence, until, soon enough, they sat in silence at the white zone, exposed to the riotous sunshine. LAX was the only airport Journeyman could imagine felt like this, a six-lane free-way up on top, the second story of the Tower of Babel. Abruptly Maddy leapt free of Todbaum's BMW, then opened the rear door and swung her titanic backpack onto the curb, before he could help. He dashed out anyhow, and said he was sorry. What if he found somewhere else for them to go? Would she stay, a day or two at least? They could go to Disneyland, he offered. Find their cous-ins in San Diego. Rent a convertible and drive the Pacific Coast Highway. She shook her head.

"It's okay, Sandy. I just—I just want to go."

"Is this something to do with the pitch?"

"What pitch?"

Journeyman was unable to keep from asking, as he'd been un-able with Todbaum, at the door. "The movie, *Yet Another World.* Peter thinks it's half yours now, apparently."

"Whatever."

"Did you talk about it?" Journeyman's bitterness crept in, an early flare of the lifelong sickness. Maddy wouldn't miss it.

"Maybe. I don't know. He can have it, I don't care. This isn't about that."

"If it isn't about this, and it isn't about that—"

"Sandy, listen now. I want you to listen."

"Tell me. Anything. I'm listening." They were inspected by a curbside checking attendant, dispassionately. The word "skycap" drifted into mind. That was what they were called. Maybe he could offer one of them the keys to the Beemer, and join Maddy in flight. It was then that she said the last thing she'd ever say to Journeyman about what had transpired between her and Peter Todbaum in the Starlet Apartments. The last thing, anyway, for some thirty years.

"He didn't do anything to me that he doesn't do to you."

"What's that? What does he do to me?"

"Sandy, don't you see?"

"What?"

"Practicing."

"Practicing? For what?" *For eating the world,* Journeyman heard himself think.

Maddy left it to Journeyman's imagination. Before turning inside she allowed him to embrace her, though without unslinging the backpack. A heartbreaking rigid embrace, such brittleness in Maddy's trapped arms, Journeyman's hands not meeting around the fullness of the pack, fingers locating instead the bulky contour of her hiking boots inside. Journeyman's eyes briefly found those of the skycap, who offered Journeyman nothing, not even a sneer; he'd witnessed too many similar scenes. Then Maddy was gone.

23.

JOURNEYMAN WAS A MIDDLE PERSON

JOURNEYMAN WAS A MIDDLE PERSON, a middleman. Always locatable between things, and therefore special witness in both directions, to extremes remote to each other, an empathic broker between irreconcilable poles—or so he flattered himself. He might only be a muddle. Mixed-up, pallid, compromised, a person ineffective and unpersuasive in all senses. He might seem an impressive writer, for instance, to civilians: he was one of those few who made his living by his pen. Yet to actual writers, when they learned that all he did was rewrite others, accept and incorporate producers' notes, and that nothing of his efforts ever got greenlit, he *wasn't* one. The proverbial writer's not-writer. Another instance: he'd loved a married person but hadn't ever been married. Now he swabbed the blood of murdered animals he'd never have been able to murder with his own hands, then delivered the resultant goods, the bacon and sausage and jerky that he'd never have been able to fashion. Nothing anchored Journeyman to any given cause or philosophy; his strategies were inconsequential, even to himself. He'd survived the Arrest by dumb luck. Even his everyday name, Sandy, placed him ambivalently: neither firmly of the land nor willing to embark offshore. Yet here he was. Offshore. In Astur's sailboat.

24.

EVERY VESSEL FINDS GROUND

JOURNEYMAN ALWAYS FORGOT. THE SEA was less a floor than
an inverted sky, the vast swallowing indifference of which he didn't
care to contemplate. Was there a name for his fear? Voluminopho-
bia? Journeyman focused instead on the network of sun-glints that
interlaced the swells, forming the illusion of a surface. Astur's boat
swept rapidly from sight of East Tinderwick, toward Quarry Island.
Nevertheless, as they turned west, the tree-break revealed the cultivated shore of Founder's Park. There, the stone wall, the gazebo, the
swing set and basketball hoop. Among these, Todbaum's car. The
Blue Streak. It too twinkled in the sun, as if made of water.

"Do you see it?" Journeyman asked her. He'd described Todbaum and the Blue Streak to her as they'd approached the dock
where she'd tethered her rowboat.

"Sure, Sandy. I see it. Did you believe you'd invented it?"

"I had some hopes."

"I'm sorry, then. Are you frightened of your friend and his machine?"

Had she read Journeyman's mind? "Shouldn't I be?" he asked
her. "Aren't *you?*"

Astur cocked her head. Indicating, Journeyman supposed, that she hadn't seen the reason yet to be afraid. She hadn't crossed the waters from the land of her birth and become a beekeeper and fallen in love with his sister and shrugged off the Arrest to be spooked so easily by Todbaum's nuclear coffeepot.

"We have to go back. I have to tell Maddy."

"I'll turn sail at the island, in the cove. The offshore wind is very strong."

"What if we blow out into the open sea?" This was a sort of fantasy. They could be the French boat in reverse, the odd couple, pointed toward the old world. A chance to suspend the judgment Journeyman felt hanging over him.

"Every vessel finds ground eventually," Astur said.

"Does the bottom of the ocean count?" Journeyman fumbled with a length of brine-smelly rope, the purpose of which eluded him, and which he couldn't have begun to be able to knot. On the water his general nonutility was made comically specific.

Astur laughed. "No, Sandy, that isn't what I meant. That isn't what I *mean*."

"Well, what do you mean?"

"Maybe your friend has something important to tell us about where he's been."

Had she intended "vessel" to include the supercar? In either case, it now felt to Journeyman that her aphorism encompassed it. So, their community was the ground that bizarre vessel had found. East Tinderwick. Founder's Park.

"There's renewed fighting elsewhere," Journeyman thought to tell her. He felt relieved to share some new information that didn't extend directly from his sojourn in Todbaum's cockpit. "Some of the Cordon guys, they're all dinged up. You know Eke? He looks rattled for a change."

"We were never going to live here forever untouched by the outside. Others have come, Sandy, don't forget. The woman in the library."

"Yes. But I *like* her."

"This is why we have to build the lighthouse."

This struck Journeyman at the time as a non sequitur. Or, at least, a merely incidental remark.

25.

LOSS

A FEW MONTHS AFTER THE Arrest's onset, Maddy got very angry with Journeyman. She'd been trying to teach him to forage for mushrooms. She'd had him briefly pegged for this role, but he was miscast. Journeyman wasn't any good at it, and shirked the opportunity. He stumbled after her on the overgrown wood paths, paused to inspect himself for imaginary ticks, was shy of snakes in the vernal pools. He forgot his training, hesitated over any identification. Perhaps it was this behavior that laid the ground for her outburst, though his behavior wasn't the subject.

The subject was loss. She felt he wasn't respectful enough of the undertow of loss in the community, in the world beyond himself. Journeyman had been complaining again about his lost relationship, compromised though it was.

"Sandy, what makes you think you're the only person who lost someone?"

He didn't think this. He tried to say so. But Maddy's words had only been the opening to a cascade. "Everyone here lost someone, we walk every day in a trench of sorrow. You imagine because you happened to be on vacation you're, like, Mr. Phantom Limb, Sandy. We're all half ghosts now."

"I didn't say—"

"You don't even have to say it, but you do. Like you're some special detector of the gone world, the sole proprietor. We *all* lost people. Parents, lovers, fucking Facebook caring circles, whatever. Nobody's special. Astur lost her entire community. She did it even before the Arrest, she's lost more than you can even imagine." After sailing to a first refuge in Yemen, Journeyman knew, Astur and her family had found passage to the Netherlands. There her brothers had remained, while Astur and her parents went on to Boston. She'd come alone to the community in Lewiston.

"I'd never try to compete with Astur," Journeyman said quietly.

"No, you compete with *me*."

"What do you mean?"

"You're Mr. Special Sad Man." Maddy veered out of control then. Journeyman could tell she was ashamed of herself, but she'd also read his mind. "I just can't stomach the self-drama, your hand-wringing, oh, woe is me, how can the mighty script doctor and adulterer have fallen to this, to killing ducks—"

"Listen—" But Journeyman had nothing. It seemed odd that he and his sister could find themselves in a contest of losses. Their most elemental wound—the lopping off of their living parents into a forever-uncertainty as to whether they'd gone on living after the Arrest—was precisely identical. If they'd suffered a degradation in their closeness, that was identical too, and reciprocal. Their bond wasn't what it had been, when they were children. It wasn't as if they never spoke, nor even that they never laughed. Still.

Only—reciprocal? He'd lost Maddy's admiration, her easy delight in his progress through life. This felt inexplicable and sad. Embarrassing. But for Maddy, her brother might have toppled from an older-sibling pedestal, starting with the disenchantment at the Starlet. Was Maddy's loss worse? Or was Journeyman's, since he had to accept the forfeiture of a sister's respect into his self-understanding? Journeyman preferred not to think about it.

II.

OCTOBER

26.

OCTOBER

THE OLD GROWTH, THE MAPLES, turned first. They rusted one leaf at a time, where ocean breezes bruised them, late in August. Paulo, the tree warden, once told Journeyman that the first trees to change reveal a map of damage. The earliest turning were those once sickened or lightning-struck. So Journeyman saw the season as a theater of succumbing. The wind's bite called each tree to solidarity with the weakest. Only the evergreens were refuseniks. Primordial trees, dinosaur trees—in their gummy hearts, they were deader than the trees that turned.

It was a season of burning leaves, burning light. Heaps of things burning. Atop the heaps, what won't burn, but only blacken and ooze: hooves, intestines, jack-o'-lanterns. Just one farm grew pumpkins anymore, enough for anyone concerned with ritual. They weren't that good to eat, after a pie or two. The Tinderwick Fair had once featured contests, pie-eating contests, but also for growing the things. Blue ribbons for swollen orange freaks, pumpkins that had to be carted in, the flesh inside no good at all.

It wasn't only smartphones and Oscar red carpet telecasts whose vanishing you could marvel over. The fairgrounds were a dusty vacancy. Why bother to go? Someone suggested all the stilled cars be hitched to horses and dragged there, Tinderwick's sole parking lot. But this was too much work. The cars rusted in ditches or fields, shrouded in weeds. Children played on them.

Journeyman sometimes thought the world had been reduced to ones, to solitaries. One farm that still grew pumpkins. One tree warden, Paulo. Paulo was the only piano tuner in the three towns, too. There was just one schoolteacher, handling the grades together, as must have been true once long ago. Journeyman's guess was fewer than forty children, fifty at most. They didn't all attend the school. Homeschooling was popular on the peninsula before the Arrest, and had carried on uninterrupted after it.

Nils repaired bicycles, and he was backed up. Journeyman tried not to be annoyed.

Needra made batches of deodorant, tampons, toothpaste, also brushes and floss. Very popular woman, Needra.

Jane and Lucius grew marijuana. The quality was incomparable, so few others troubled with personal plants. Mostly they were busy farming potatoes, tomatoes, kale.

One butcher, one butcher's assistant and mop-up man. Victoria made sausages.

Andy, the one psychiatrist. He carried on as before, though he was paid now in what resembled charity or tribute: dinners from the farmers; refurbished shoes from our shoe refurbisher, Osgood, who seemed to need a lot of therapy. Andy had been known to give away the extra shoes.

Of course this wasn't strictly true. Frequently they had more than one of everything. Other times, none. For instance, no politician. Renate, Tinderwick's mayor before, stepped down, returned to her work as a veterinarian. No one took her place. They had no policeman. This ought to be concerning, but wasn't. The town's policeman hadn't been a Tinderwick resident anyway, but lived in Snowport. After the Arrest he'd joined the Cordon. They had no criminal, that

Journeyman knew of. Not in the sense of a pickpocket or mugger anyway.

They had no storyteller. Journeyman hadn't had to decline the position. No one asked.

They'd had one monster, and sent him to the Lake of Tiredness. There wasn't room for another.

27.

THE FIRST STORY

PETER TODBAUM WAS OUT OF his protective capsule. Why shouldn't he be? It was a beautiful day. Todbaum had expanded his little fiefdom at Founder's Park to include the gazebo and picnic table by the water. He placed his back to the water, Journeyman supposed, so he could keep his eye on the Blue Streak, and track who approached the park from the road, as Journeyman did now.

Theodore Nowlin sat with Todbaum there under the gazebo's shade, erect and stern in his usual way, his posture claiming puritan virtue and rectitude. Yet his eyes were dazzled, rapt. Journeyman had seen that drunken look before, on other faces. It came about when Todbaum's mouth started moving.

Another man sat with them, one Journeyman didn't know. Not a man, quite, Journeyman realized as he approached. A teenager. Journeyman recalled a set of teenage-boy twins, part of the off-the-grid, backroads community deep in East Tinderwick's interior land, only occasionally sighted in town. This was one of them.

As Journeyman got nearer, he saw that Todbaum had given his listeners espresso. A little coffee picnic, out under the gazebo's shade, here at the end of the world. It would be the first coffee the teenager had ever tasted.

"—whole state's a protectorate," Todbaum was saying. "Sure, sure, you might think your local survivalist squads have a franchise, a leg up, but let me tell you, nobody's got anything on these Mormons; they're like *fiends* of competency, been drawing up blueprints for apocalyptic eventualities since the day they handed those golden plates back to the angel Moroni. Howard Hughes put himself in Mormon hands for a reason. You know from Howard Hughes?"

The teenager looked at him blankly.

"Richest man in the world, inventor of the underwire brassiere, he's like the patron saint of American paranoids. He used the Mormons like his own private CIA, only at some point it might have been that the operatives were running him as a figurehead, who knows? I wouldn't put it past them. When I rolled through there was just one quadrant of Utah they hadn't placed under their dominion. I mean, one quadrant worth having, resource-wise—a lot of that place is a wasteland, salt flats, nothing arable or habitable, particularly, nothing cattle can graze, but there's orchards at the right altitudes—ever had a Utah apple?"

"Good apples," said Theodore Nowlin, gravely.

"Great apples," said Todbaum. "I rolled out of there with a basket of Fujis, kept me alive halfway into Nebraska. I should have been hoarding the pips, if I was smarter. You people would have known what to do with them. Hey, Sandman, you need a coffee?"

"I'm okay," Journeyman said. He'd stopped his bicycle near enough, to place a cheesecloth-wrapped package on the table beside them. A spelt loaf. But he stayed on the bicycle.

"You off to see Madeleine?"

"Well, yes."

"Say hi to her for me. Or no, on second thought, don't." This was a running joke between them now, or a running joke between Todbaum and Todbaum. "I want to surprise her."

Todbaum had been here ten days now without yet seeing Journeyman's sister.

"Okay."

He went back to his story. "There's a private corporation, with a whole campus dug up in the Oquirrh mountain range. There's freshwater streams up there, totally self-sustaining, and it's practically a mini-cult, a corporate cult, like they've beat the Mormons at their own game. Drives 'em crazy, too, having this secret holding just beyond their control. Place is called White Walnut. So, after I got into my dealings with the Mormons, they entreated me to use the Blue Streak to go up there, and would you believe it, the persuasiveness of these guys, and, also, I was getting a little intrigued, like what if they've got what I've got—nuclear turbines? What if they've got something I *don't*? So, I started up the mountain. Only White Walnut's shrouded. Complete and utter mystery to me how they did this."

"What do you mean by *shrouded*?" asked Theodore Nowlin, with excited irritation.

"Just what you think I'd mean. They're invisible, in a sense. There's this opaque fog, when you approach their altitude. Just the whole place is shrouded. I don't know if they can see through it, or how they navigated blind, but I sure couldn't—"

Journeyman took off. The story disturbed him in any number of ways. But before he could dwell on it, he noticed what he hadn't before: two children, a boy and a girl, clambering on the Blue Streak's exterior. The boy, on the ladder to the hatch. Journeyman felt a pitch of anxiety in his stomach, recalling Todbaum's description of the dilating blades that protected the entry point. But the boy didn't attempt to enter, just perched. Perhaps the girl had begun on the ladder too, but she'd spidered around, in her tattery dress, and clung instead to a vertical vent that resembled a set of giant shark's gills, nearer to the bare gleaming engine rods. The children turned, noticing Journeyman noticing them. Both were barefoot. Journeyman believed they were the younger siblings of the teenage twin who sat with Todbaum beneath the gazebo. He wished he could remember the family's name, so he could ask Maddy about them. Did their parents know they were here? But such questions might be, as they used to say with giddy frequency in Journeyman's former life, above his pay grade.

28.

JOURNEYMAN'S ROUNDS
HAD EXPANDED

JOURNEYMAN'S ROUNDS HAD EXPANDED. NILS, exasperatingly, had not fixed his bicycle, but he'd loaned Journeyman a spare. He needed it. After his morning duties at the butcher's, then delivering the caul and scrap to Victoria, and gathering from her some finished product, his round of farms and recipients had grown. He brought care packages to the Lake of Tiredness, also to the woman in the library—and now, all the way back to East Tinderwick, to Todbaum. For in some unofficial way, by grudging consent, Todbaum had been approved as a ward of the towns. While what he might contribute had yet to be determined, he'd be fed.

29.

THE WOMAN WHO LIVED
IN THE LIBRARY

THE START HAD BEEN INNOCUOUS. It was several weeks, perhaps a month, before Todbaum's arrival in the supercar. The butcher,
Augustus Cordell, said to Journeyman, "A woman moved into the
library."

Journeyman felt mild surprise. "From where?"

Augustus shrugged. "She left a rowboat at the golf course landing." Behind the country club's overgrown golf course lay a short
beach that was nearly useless as a boat landing—useless because
there were no moorings and because it was walled from the road, so
nothing larger than what might be carried, a plastic kayak at most,
would put in there.

"She rowed here?"

He shrugged again. Augustus was not one to speculate.

"She doesn't know anyone?"

"The folks at Proscenium Farm asked me to bring her something to eat, but they didn't know her name. Maybe you ought to
include her in your rounds this week."

"Well, sure." This was as near as the community might come to
a general proclamation of welcome, but also a request to declare

one's purposes: Here's a basket of sausage, bread, and preserves. Now, where do you see yourself in a week or a month? The butcher also knew that Journeyman cherished visiting the empty library. In this he was scarcely alone. Journeyman's first thought was that this rowing woman shouldn't screw up such an essential part of the post-Arrest commons.

She'd barred the doors from within, so he had to pound on them, and call out, and wait. Yet when she opened them it was without demanding he identify himself. She seemed more irked than afraid.

"Yes?"

"I have food for you."

"Who sent you?"

"No one. It's just what we do."

"Okay, thank you."

"I'm Alexander Duplessis."

"Okay, that's good to know."

"We—a lot of people like to come in here and get books."

"Is there a particular book you want today?"

Are you a librarian? he almost said. "Sometimes I don't know what I'm looking for until I find it."

"That's a luxurious attitude, these days."

"Well, you've come to a place of . . . I don't know if I'd call it *luxury*, exactly. But we do find time for certain pleasures." Was he being flirtatious? Would she notice if he was? "I mean like looking at the books in the library."

"It's a lucky place," she said. "Do you even know how lucky?"

"No, I'm sure I don't." Journeyman waited for her to say where she'd come from in her rowboat, or whether that had even been her rowboat.

"You shouldn't leave a place like this unguarded."

"The library, you mean?"

"I'll keep watch over it now."

In this tautological way, she'd revealed just what the butcher might have deputized Journeyman to learn: that in exchange for food, the woman in the library would provide the service of being the woman in the library.

"Will you tell me your name?" he said.

"Another time."

"Okay."

30.

THE SECOND STORY

"—WHO SHOULD I FIND BUT a couple of minor, washed-up tabloid stars holding court there, king and queen of the goddamn prom. Really, these two couldn't get a meeting—couldn't get arrested in my town anymore. But we've all got some form of luck; this turned out to be theirs. They'd been doing a road show deal, playing the *we-really-love-doing-theater* card, so they were in Cheyenne, Wyoming, of all the godforsaken places, when the whole thing shook down, instead of trapped with everybody else in L.A. Before, if you'd busted them out in Podunk they'd be begging you not to mention it to anybody. Now they had this whole place wrapped around their finger because of their cornpone charisma and Botox-frozen mugs imprinted on brains by endless tired reruns on AMC. Fame is a fucking currency, my friends—"

This might not actually have been the second story. It was the second Journeyman heard. He didn't stay to hear more. He had rounds to complete. Theodore Nowlin was with Todbaum again, and the teenager too, but this time the circle had grown: Here was Mike Raritan, listening as well. Victoria had come. And Nils. Shouldn't Nils be fixing bicycles? Well, he wasn't. He was drinking Todbaum's coffee. Todbaum doled out coffee from the Blue Streak to anyone who cared to drop by.

31.

BY THE TIME MADDY
WENT TO FOUNDER'S PARK

ONCE IT HAD BEEN MORE than a week, Journeyman felt it, a metronome of anxiety in his chest. He felt it at each stop on his rounds, his retracing of that benign morning in September, when he'd first been surprised by the Cordon on the road, when he'd re-entered the towns as captive or guest in the splendid atrocious machine. Each day bent around the question: when *would* his sister go to see Peter Todbaum and his car?

At the very start, that Tuesday afternoon, after returning with Astur on her boat and walking in to find Maddy at the Farm, his sister had forbade Todbaum's visiting Spodosol. Forbade in the most casual sense of the word. When Journeyman explained that Todbaum had called the Farm his destination, she'd waved her hand. Barely coming out of her crouch as she picked aphids from the underleaves of her staked tomato vines, she'd only said, "Well, he can't come here."

Journeyman wanted witnesses. Astur stood talking with Renee and Ernesto in the far corner of the greenhouse. Renee, before the Arrest, had been a solitary housepainter and handyperson. In its wake she'd fallen in love with the younger Ernesto, one of the ex-berry-pickers and a founder of the tamale concern, and come to learn farming. The two were industrious and inseparable, seeming born for this new world. But these other Spodosolians—Astur, Renee, Ernesto—had seemingly overheard nothing. For Journeyman to be the sole hearer of his sister's injunction was to be tasked, he felt, with enforcing it.

At the same time, their presence meant he couldn't plead with Maddy for forgiveness for having led Todbaum here. Not just now. Instead, Journeyman tried to match his sister's impassive tone.

"Of course he won't."

"He can stay in the park for now."

Her imperturbability amazed Journeyman. It was almost as though she'd been expecting Todbaum.

"Sure," he hedged. What would keep the Blue Streak anywhere if it didn't want to be kept? Had Todbaum even really been a captive of the Cordon men who'd escorted him down the road? Or had he been using them as a presidential motorcade uses the Secret Service? "And then what?"

She shrugged. "Well, it depends, Sandy, doesn't it? On what he wants."

"He said he wants to live here."

She turned to him, then, and smiled. "Who wouldn't?"

That was all for that day. They moved to other topics.

Journeyman had expected that it might be a day or two before she condescended to visit Todbaum. In his projections they'd go together, he and his sister, perhaps with Astur too, or others from the Farm. A contingent, not a posse. He was mistaken. A week went by, then another.

He imagined, then, that she might be organizing some kind of quasi-official response, an ad hoc committee for welcome or unwelcome. Though Journeyman spent more time there since Todbaum's arrival, he certainly didn't know everything that went on in East Tinderwick. He ate dinner two or three nights a week at Spodosol, yet hardly heard every scheme hashed out in a commons room or fireside, late at night, after he'd left.

He was wrong in this too. Maddy let everyone guess just as she let Journeyman guess—and Todbaum as well. Power accrued to her by this act of omission, her air of nonconcern. The longer she didn't visit Todbaum, the more certain that others besides Journeyman would see her response to his arrival as the crucial, the defining one. A chess game. The longer East Tinderwick's queen refused to budge, the more helpless the other pieces were revealed to be.

Yet it seemed to Journeyman that Todbaum accrued a kind of power too, in his own nonbudging way. People were weirdly drawn to him, as they had always been. Children and teenagers, and Theodore Nowlin. Those who longed for the lost world of machines. Todbaum had this thing they wanted to touch and see, the Blue Streak. It worked like a magnet. The absence of any consensus about Todbaum and his machine, the post-Arrest unmediating and unbundling of human opinion, was also a clarion: one had to go see for oneself.

After nightfall, the thing was radiant too. It was as though a television set had been switched on in a valley of the moon.

By the time Maddy went to Founder's Park she was the last to go. No, that wasn't strictly true. There were those no more interested than they'd be if the East Tinderwick Village Improvement Society had erected a new methane-powered stoplight in front of the old post office. Some, the back-roaders, shunned the center of town. These were those who'd anticipated and preempted the Arrest, who tried to go the Arrest one better. They prided themselves not only on their self-reliance but on their self-circumscription to a cultural time and space that barely acknowledged an "elsewhere" or "before." Like the clambering kids, they were often barefoot, in as few clothes as weather allowed. Knowledge of Todbaum's arrival, if it reached them, was foreclosed to their curiosity. Another dumb blip of the civilization of the always-mistaken.

Others in Tinderwick, and especially in Granite Head, might have regarded it as too far to travel. Not being bicyclists or horse riders, they'd make do with gossip for now. Perhaps they'd inspect the supercar the next time they had a cause to be out that way. Still, among East Tinderwick's wider population, those who could be seen at a meeting or a barn dance, all had made their way down to Founder's Park before Maddy. All had gone for at least a middle-distance gawk at the machine. Many had gone closer. Many of those who'd gone closer had stayed awhile. They'd stayed to sample Todbaum's espresso and balderdash, or to hear one of his stories of what lay outside their benign perimeter, the things he'd encountered in his crossing.

When Journeyman couldn't bear it any longer, he tried to explain this to Maddy. "He's making friends out of your friends," Journeyman said. "You know how he can be."

"I think I remember," Maddy said. They were in her kitchen. Her hands were busy as usual, feeding cobs through a hand-cranked sheller to grind off the hardened kernels. Her latest project, popcorn. "Something like flavor of the month, every month. Whether anyone actually likes the flavor or not."

"The thing is, I think some people might like the flavor," said Journeyman. "Any novelty in a vacuum."

"Good," said Maddy, indecipherably. "Good for him, and good for them."

"He's begun scheduling these things now. It's threatening to become a ritual. Mike Raritan has been building fires in the pit, and making those weird fake s'mores of his." These were actually delicious, accompanied by a fresh Blue Streak espresso and the scent of smoke wafting into the stars above the island.

"Scheduling what things?"

"His narrational sessions, his rallies. It's like a political campaign." Journeyman realized he himself was campaigning, to arouse his sister's concern.

"People need ritual," Maddy agreed. One of her conversational judo moves. Journeyman felt chagrined, as if he'd gone to the office hours of his anthropology professor and tried to interest him in the games of beer pong back at his dorm.

"It's more than ritual, maybe," he proposed. "Some of us have been waiting for word from . . . outside . . . for a while."

Now Maddy grinned. "Others of us go outside every single day. Like me, now. Dodie Metzger said she found some matsutake in the woods just off the Drunkard's Path the other day."

"What's—?" He didn't pretend to try to pronounce it.

"A mushroom, the best mushroom. It's that season again. Want to come with me?"

Journeyman begged off. He had deliveries still to make. He was ashamed of his failure to become the town's mushroom forager.

Journeyman's final attempt to interest Maddy in the situation at the park was halfway successful. "There's more kids climbing on that thing every day it seems. You should see them, Maddy."

"I've heard. He's a regular pied piper." He'd found his sister in her hammock with a book, one he'd recommended to her, actually. *Earth Abides*, by George R. Stewart. The book was open, face-down, nestled between elbow and ribs. A few orange maple leaves had fallen and stuck to her sweater. Journeyman gave the hammock a soft push.

"He's not encouraging them, that I can see. But he doesn't do anything to discourage them, either."

"What are you trying to say, Sandy?" she asked sharply. "That he's going to hurt the kids?"

"I didn't say that. But the machine is powered by some kind of fuel rods. He sleeps in a lead-lined vault up in there. It could be dangerous."

"It's probably safer than swimming in the quarries," she said, crossly. A child had died in one of the granite quarries two years earlier.

"Sure."

"A lot of things are dangerous."

"Sure, Maddy. I know."

"I'm not in charge of anyone's kids."

"Of course. So, did you hear about the tent?"

"What tent?"

At last Journeyman's news seemed to surprise her. "Just into the tree line, east of the park, there's a tent. A camp, really. It looks like a hunter's camp, like with a deer blind." Journeyman didn't know exactly what he was talking about.

"Whose camp?"

"You remember Eke? He was part of the team that brought Todbaum in that day. Him and some other Cordon guy I don't recognize." In fact, Journeyman had barely glimpsed either person. He knew it was Eke only because Paulo had told him so.

"Are they doing anything?"

"Not that anyone can see. Just sort of staking Todbaum out. I guess they've been at the water a few times, fishing. They're not really trying to stay hidden, but they don't come hang out, either, at least not while I was around. Not during the stories."

"Someone needs to go talk to them."

"Maybe so."

"I'll go down there," she said, at last.

"You want me to—"

"No. I'll go alone."

32.

THE EIGHTH OR TENTH STORY

JOURNEYMAN COULDN'T KNOW WHETHER IT was the eighth or the tenth or some other number. There'd been plenty. He'd caught parts of at least three others, and knew he'd missed more. He'd never learned the finish of the tale of Utah, of the Mormons and the strange opaque fog cloaking the corporate redoubt in the mountains—it had gone on and on. When he'd asked some of its hearers to retell it, he found it changing in their retelling. Attenuating, growing strange and hopeless, as though only Todbaum could tell it right. The tale itself was enclosed in an opaque fog, perhaps.

Journeyman had pulled over on his way home from Spodosol, late that same day when he'd finally triggered Maddy's alarm, finally gained her attention. He'd been riding his loaner bicycle when he saw the campfire's sparks rising past the silhouetted treetops, to the pale-clouded moon. A good crowd was gathered, more than Journeyman had seen there before. He hoped to hang at the periphery, in the dark, and listen without being singled out as he sometimes was by Todbaum. He felt the chance his sister might not be far behind him, that she was reckoning an approach to the new world of Founder's Park. If Maddy came, he'd watch and learn what went on between them. It seemed his responsibility, now that he'd finally instigated it.

Todbaum was just underway. "If I learned one thing coming across, it was watch the fuck out for the sole town in the middle of absolute zippo nowhere. Worse than the inner-city blues, worse than suburban sprawl, the strips where nothing was the same more than two or three miles at a time even though it all *looked* the same. The tiny towns were worse, even, than the big-perimeter formats, the gated zones. Because within the castle walls, the folks with the guns and underground storage tanks, however many corny fascist scripts they're working through, however much they're still jerking off to Reddit memes about George Soros—once they've carved off their piece of turf they're also sort of playing *Minecraft*, or maybe it's *The Sims*. You know, feed the people, enforce the rules, balance the little ecosystem. Every man a wife or two, nobody goes hungry on my watch, that kind of crap. Like—" Here, Todbaum lowered his voice to a theatrical hush and glanced at the tree line. There the two men in the tent, Eke and his friend, harbored near to their own fire, which glowed a faint orange. "Like your neighbors to the south."

Journeyman crept nearer. He scanned the faces lit not only by the firelight but by its intricate reflection off the Blue Streak's chromework. So many he recognized, so many he didn't. Among them, Sophie Thurber and Edwin Gorse were new apparitions, unexpected to see, perhaps to be interpreted as signs. Sophie Thurber was the spinster matriarch of the Thurber's Corner houses. Her surname featured on dozens of stones in the Tinderwick cemetery, provenance on the peninsula. Yet, unlike Theodore Nowlin, Sophie Thurber was no meeting attender, not a rallier to causes, spoke to barely anyone. She reputedly had a miser's fortune tucked into her home's walls, a thing now only theoretical, or virtual. A fortune in dry strike-anywhere matches would be better. Who, Journeyman wondered, had managed to interest Sophie in the doings at Founder's Park? And how? A mystery.

Edwin Gorse was another thing entirely. An inventor of some

cash-cow pharmaceutical, he'd two years before the Arrest taken early retirement and bought one of the old money-sucking mansions crumbling on Tinderwick's High Street. He cleaned it up, then moved in his family, wife and two young girls, while apparently knowing no one on the peninsula. Not that they wouldn't have found a welcome place here, or shouldn't have. The towns embraced what used to be called "transplants"—as opposed to summer people. Yet when he was Arrest-widowed—his wife away on a business trip—Gorse and his daughters turned inward, shunning the new all-ages school, living behind a hedge. To pull his weight he tilled the old house's grand lawn and made himself into an expert potato farmer. Journeyman found him a bit of a cold fish. Yet now he'd found his way to Todbaum's campfire. Journeyman found himself thinking of the two girls, a town away, alone in the tall gingerbready house. Perhaps Gorse had hired a babysitter. Perhaps the oldest girl was old enough now to look after the younger. What did Journeyman know about children?

"So, Paper Moon, Kansas, was dead in the prairie wastes, a pin in the map of nowhere. If you think Kansas was dull driving when it was all corn and 'only two hundred miles to Kickapoo moccasin and fudge emporium,' you should catch it now. I saw signs of life and pulled over—my bad. I think I might have glimpsed the worst brainwash nightmare cult I ever saw in that fucking town, and I saw a few. It was an egg cult. Yeah, you heard me right."

Journeyman glanced again in the direction of the tent in the woods, the cigarette-tip flare of their campfire. He imagined he could detect the scent, a good one, of fish the camping men had caught and grilled over their coals. Todbaum had lowered his voice unnecessarily, to match the scant wind in the trees, the crackle and murmur and faint surf. All Journeyman could make out from within this circle of light was the Cordon men's fire—who was to say they'd stayed beside it, not slipped nearer, as Journeyman had done himself?

"They had a giant egg, rigged up by the side of the railroad tracks. Three or four stories tall, painted like an Easter egg, old-world style. 'World's Largest Czech Egg, Paper Moon, Kansas' it read on the side. And there was more fucking barbwire around that thing, and guard towers, like the Berlin Wall—picture a town split at the railroad tracks, and the Czech egg was Checkpoint Charlie. And it *had* been a chicken town, and still was. Those monstrous industrial chicken factory buildings, you know the kind of thing. Ten thousand chickens, each in a ten-inch cell, no light, no contact, just machines tending them, eggs rolling down a trap chute. If this town was Berlin, the chickens were the ones in the concentration camps, I guess. Only the whole thing breaks down without an industrial-level power source, ventilation, all the automated feed machines, what have you. You can't exactly run a ten-thousand-chicken barracks off of bicycle power or solar panels, not that they had any of those anyhow. Strictly gas or diesel operation, dead in the water. So they'd freed all the chickens on the side of the tracks where the men and the guns were. They let 'em roost in the vacant downtown, variety store, boarded-up movie palace, all the businesses that had died probably fifty years before the Arrest, the old American story. Chickens everywhere, pecking at rocks, eating each other's dead bodies. Before you ask, I never once saw cannibalism, coming across, not once. I'm not saying there *isn't* any, I'm just not stupid enough to pilot myself into precincts dire enough for a close-up. Never saw cannibalism, apart from the chicken cannibalism in Paper Moon, Kansas. What the *people* ate was eggs, day and night. And the ones with the guns and the wire on the north side of the tracks, the men of the Czech egg, they took petitions at the fence. Starving, sorry-ass people from miles around were at that fence, trading anything— canned cat food, sexual favors—for those free-range ghost-town cannibal-chicken eggs. It wasn't my favorite locale, let's just say."

Todbaum still held it, Journeyman had to admit. The conch shell, the horn of story. Still, Journeyman had to find his way home to the other town, in the dark. As he mounted his bicycle, he felt the irksome echo of Todbaum's voice in his ear, in his brain. Was it only Journeyman's imagination, or had Todbaum drifted into doing his impression of Journeyman's voice?

Maybe Todbaum had no instrument of his own. Maybe he'd conjured up the only voice he had by melding his father's browbeating tone and Journeyman's dorky plaint, shored up by scraps of Jack Nicholson, Christopher Walken, whomever else. Journeyman shook off this thought, bicycled away.

Madeleine hadn't come.

33.

FOOTAGE, NAPKIN

THE NEXT AFTERNOON TODBAUM HAD Journeyman up to his cockpit to learn of his sister's visit. Rather than explain, Todbaum showed him the footage captured by the Blue Streak's security camera. He cued to the start of the action easily, as if he'd been watching it repeatedly that morning before Journeyman appeared.

The lens was fish-eyed, panoramic. Maddy loomed into the center abruptly, after seeming at first to peel around the image's perimeter. She carried a ladder. This was in darkness, by moonlight, though the camera's superior capacity rendered everything clear, as if shot with some day-for-night lens. The scene was free of other actors, the gathering dissolved, the fire now just embers, Maddy alone. It was a painter's folding ladder she employed, perhaps eighteen or twenty feet long. Tools hung at her belt. She moved nearer the camera, unfolded the ladder, tested its placement alongside the Blue Streak. Though she'd chosen not to climb the outside of the vehicle itself, which suggested caution—or distaste?—she appeared unconcerned that she'd triggered any alarms, or, indeed, that the camera eye recorded her actions. She moved with steady purpose.

When Maddy was an arm's length from the cockpit dome, she

reached for what dangled from her tool belt. A simple claw hammer. With no hesitation, no gentle test strike, she reared the hammer back over her shoulder, then slammed its head against the transparent dome. A second time, even harder. Then again. She rained steady blows, with no obvious result. It was at this moment, however, that Todbaum, presumably startled from sleep by the hammer's assault, must have come from his lead-lined sleeping vault, into the dome. Maddy waved. She smiled, tight-lipped. And went on hammering.

Was Todbaum now trying to get her attention? Screaming at her? There was no audio. She raised her eyebrows slightly, smiling again. She holstered the hammer, but only to reach for the other tool at her waist. A blowtorch, a small one. From it she sparked a white-blue flame, a tiny blade of light, and applied it to the curve of the dome. Her brow was furrowed with intent, yet amusement played on her lips.

Again, the dome didn't give. She holstered the blowtorch. Now Journeyman saw her respond to something. Was Todbaum yelling at her? Maddy showed only passing irritation, not granting him her full attention, and descended the ladder. She folded it again and started back across the moonlit grass.

This was the whole of Maddy's inquiries at Founder's Park. With no apparent result. Except now Todbaum pulled a scrap of paper napkin from his pocket.

"She's good, I'll give her that."

"Good at what?"

Todbaum shoved the napkin into Journeyman's hands. Journeyman saw it was covered with Todbaum's scrawl. His wretched handwriting. In the years they'd worked together Todbaum had used it only to make indecipherable jottings in the margins of scripts, and to sign checks.

"What is this?"

"A proposal—a contract, really. All she has to do is sign. You'll be the witness. Me and her are working together again, if we ever really stopped."

"Working on what?"

"On this." Todbaum spread his hands, indicating—everything. "*Yet Another World*. We can name it with some literary allusion, if you like—*The Figure in the Carpet . . . The Serpent . . . O Rose, Thou Art Sick*, whatever. I always figured our title was just a placeholder anyway."

"You think you're making a movie?"

"Way bigger than a movie, Sandy. Me and Maddy, we're jump-starting history, the whole tentpole franchise. Dystopia and post-apocalypse, two great tastes that taste great together. The rupture, me and her, that's the problem, right? So, it's also the solution. Last night she let me know she knows."

Journeyman examined the napkin. Only stray phrases were legible at a glance. *Fractured FRACTAL reality breakdowns = partitions: fractal daze days/STASIS v. DYNAMISM*—with that, Journeyman quit trying to parse them. Another quadrant of the napkin was cross-hatched with columns of numbers. Todbaum had been breaking down the budget, perhaps. Or proposing the splits.

"She's meant to . . . sign this napkin?"

"Why not? I signed. C'mon, Sandman, where's your sense of destiny? All the immortal deals go down on cocktail napkins. The Gettysburg Address was written on a candy wrapper five minutes before Abe got onstage. I exaggerate."

Todbaum exaggerated.

Journeyman put the napkin in his pocket.

34.

JOURNEYMAN TOOK
A DISCO NAP

JOURNEYMAN DIDN'T PRESENT TODBAUM'S NAPKIN to his sister. It remained captive in his pocket through the following day, a flaming tendril of Todbaum's madness.

Why should Journeyman be the go-between? He knew the answer: he'd fated himself for this role the day he steered the supercar to Founder's Park, if not decades before. He'd asked to be the middle person. He shouldn't want it any other way.

Journeyman had never made it to the end of one of Todbaum's stories. The doings in Founder's Park ground on past his ordinary bedtime. There was usually a kind of question and answer period. Or Todbaum would restart, elaborate, keeping his listeners enspelled. Journeyman saw them in town the mornings after, wandering as if hungover.

Journeyman needed to know more. If he'd accepted his appointment as intermediary—he saw no way to refuse it—he should grasp the goings-on at the park. Who left last? Was the fire extinguished or did it die? Would Maddy return? Journeyman took what in his former life was called a disco nap. He'd bedded down at dusk for a few hours, then rode back in the dark—Nils had finally completed repairs on his bicycle.

Was this the fourteenth story? The twentieth? Journeyman arrived for the finish. He hid his bicycle in the woods and clung in the gloom at the edge of the park. Another moonless night. He counted just three heads at the fire, the last faithful. Theodore Nowlin's craggy figure, unmistakable. Journeyman couldn't identify the others. Todbaum talked with his hands, outlined in the campfire's flame. The Blue Streak flickered in the firelight. The wind knocked down Todbaum's voice before it reached his hiding place, but Journeyman felt he could follow the tale by his gesticulations. Perhaps this was Journeyman's training rising to the surface, after years taking Todbaum's dictation and notes. He shivered, wishing he could move to the fire.

Finally the last three were gone. Todbaum sat alone. Journeyman's urge to reveal himself and discover what Todbaum would choose to say struggled against the urge to remain hidden and learn what Todbaum might not want him to know, or didn't know. Journeyman waited.

Two men came out of the woods nearer the shore, startling Journeyman. Eke and his friend. They'd had no fire themselves this night. Perhaps they hadn't even been in their camp before appearing here. Todbaum greeted them familiarly, it looked to Journeyman. He seemed at least unthreatened. The two stood by the fire. Todbaum ascended the ladder of the Blue Streak, returning with something, and handed a part of the something to each of them, which they accepted. Cups. Then poured from another part of the something, a tall pour from a bottle or thermos. Had Todbaum lied about his exhausted supply of scotch? Or was it coffee?

Night coffee.

Journeyman wanted some himself but kept to his hiding place.

Todbaum climbed back into his cockpit. Eke and his friend stood a moment, close at the fire, drinking what he'd given them.

Then they began to shed their clothing. Journeyman watched, trying to believe. He didn't need to believe for it to occur: it did. The two bearded young men stripped bare, leaving their clothes in a single pile, and moved nearer to the fire. One tossed on additional fuel, from the wood gathered there, the wood Todbaum's constituency had brought with them as tribute, from their own hard-won supplies. The two naked men began to dance.

They were not skilled dancers, Journeyman thought. But inspired. They capered near the flames to warm themselves. They also danced fully around the Blue Streak's circumference, danced in mad fascination, it seemed to Journeyman, paying the vehicle homage with their bodies, daring themselves to touch it, as if it were hot. The glow in the impermeable cockpit faded, leaving only the supercar's general luminosity. If Todbaum was watching, he sat in the dark. The dance went on.

When it ended, it ended with two bodies on the trampled grass and softened ground nearest the dying fire. One—he couldn't tell them apart—sucked the other's penis. Journeyman shrank deeper into his cold nest of leaves. He couldn't move, frozen by the chill and by his embarrassment. He didn't budge until they'd reclothed and departed for their own camp beyond the tree line. By the time he'd gone, the fire was cold, embers dimmed to black. The last illumination, this moonless night, was the supercar's own gentle and persistent incandescence. It drew a thick fog of moths, mosquitoes, hairy fliers of all types.

Night coffee.

Gay Cordon sex.

Oh, the doings in Founder's Park.

35.

JOURNEYMAN SOMETIMES TRIED TO THINK ABOUT THE CORDON

THE TOWNS HAD NEVER HAD exiles from the Cordon before. Had the two men come to live in the woods near the park because their mutual desire made them unwelcome? Or was that unfair to the Cordon? Journeyman had no idea.

If it was the case, if they'd come for solidarity, they could have sought out Nils. Or others—even Maddy and Astur. Not made their strange encampment near Todbaum. Could the entire Cordon offer them no example?

Journeyman sometimes tried to think about the Cordon and found it difficult. The audience for Todbaum's stories attested to the insatiability, among Journeyman's neighbors, for pictures of what lay outside their sphere. Even those who'd lost little in the Arrest craved wider news. Then there was the Cordon: a close example of people other than themselves. A group, a region, organized otherwise. The Cordon people hid in plain sight, irritants to be endured, appetites to be fed.

You could say a few things with confidence: That they were content with the bargain they'd struck, uninterested in acquiring the skills they lacked.

That they advertised their willingness to do violence and wore disdain on their sleeves, but weren't gratuitous.

That they allowed some traffic, yet were unwilling to transmit news or description. That those from the towns who'd crossed into the Cordon region—many, in the early days—never returned, but few feared the Cordon had chosen to do them harm.

That they believed in the standard of necessity—their own, above all.

Otherwise, there was something mute or inchoate about the Cordon. In their stubbornness they seemed even to refuse Journeyman's curiosity. He suspected he wasn't alone in this.

36.

WE LOSE OURSELVES

KORMENTZ HAD BEGUN TO INSIST on reading to Journeyman from his *Pillow Book* in progress, fresh wearisome pages concerning things like the play of late October light on the surface of the lake. Today he unveiled a passage that made a kind of litany out of the phrase *we lose ourselves*. He insisted Journeyman sit with him by the water while he read it, crinkling his pages of neat tiny cursive, bugging his fish-eyes at Journeyman for approval between each line. As he piled up renditions of how we were *losing ourselves*, Journeyman nearly lost it.

"We lose ourselves lately, in these unnumbered days / We lose ourselves in our tasks and our friends / And in making amends / We lose ourselves in ourselves / And in the art of losing / And in the setting down in lines of what we've lost / In these unnumbered days—"

"Jerome, hey, sorry."

"Yes?"

Journeyman fantasized he drove a bulldozer, to plow Kormentz and his sententious poem into the lake, there never to be heard from again. "I have to go, I've got deliveries to make. And there's a big meeting today."

"It's just a little longer. I've got tasks as well."

"I really can't stay." Journeyman wanted to scream. *What tasks?* Kormentz had none. But something else bothered Journeyman: these days no longer seemed to him unnumbered. The arrival of Todbaum and his machine had, precisely, *renumbered* them.

Journeyman thrust his hands into his pocket, found Todbaum's napkin. He could draw it out and read it to baffle Kormentz. Claim it was a poem or koan. But no. On the whole peninsula just one person remained unquestionably innocent of Todbaum's arrival: Kormentz. Better it stay that way. Journeyman extricated himself. If he wanted a confidant, he should visit the library again, to try and call on the woman who'd installed herself there. In fact, he resolved to do it today, after the meeting.

Yet like a bad song Kormentz's lyric invested itself in Journeyman's head. Through the rest of the day, right into the specially convened meeting with the contingent from the Cordon, he found himself cobbling variations upon it: *We lose ourselves in our stories / And in washing the blood from our hands / We lose ourselves in guessing / Who's lying to us or themselves / And in lying to them / And to ourselves—*

37.

A BIG MEETING, PART 1

THE TOWNS ASSEMBLED GOODS FOR the Cordon—ripe vegetables, sacks of grain, cloth-wrapped cheese, sausage and jerky, jars of what had been pickled or preserved or fermented or distilled, a steam-sealed wax-paper pack of tamales—in a weekly Friday afternoon drop at the North Grange Hall. It was more than Journeyman could carry alone. Others helped, by horse and bicycle. Still, he was the designated go-between. Though others dropped off goods, Journeyman often was the only one present for the exchange, apart from Quentin Maslow, who lived alone in the upstairs of the Grange.

Quentin, like Journeyman, had been a houseguest on the peninsula at the time of the Arrest. An odd, shy bird, likely also a malingering depressive, he clearly couldn't stay with his hosts permanently after. Quentin lacked even the thread of familial connection Journeyman benefited from, in Maddy and her farm; he hardly appeared to like his former friends in Tinderwick. Quentin conveyed an air of not-caring that his own life had become such a marginal thing. He smoked a great deal of Jane and Lucius's excellent marijuana, and often got Journeyman high when he arrived for the Cordon's pickup.

He'd managed the Grange Hall, such as it required managing.
Quentin served, Journeyman supposed, as an informal perimeter
sentry for the three towns, the first to see what came down the central road—not that he would likely be able to do anything about it.
He certainly hadn't raced down to inform anyone of the arrival of
the Blue Streak, on that consequential Tuesday. Quentin frequently
sat in on the exchanges with the Cordon folk as they loaded the
towns' offerings, though he rarely spoke a word.

Others stayed away. In Journeyman's estimate, his neighbors
preferred not to confront the fact that their safety was mortgaged
by regular installments of precious food. The fact that their farms
were in a sense plantations. No love was lost on either side. The
Cordon people who arrived to receive the goods compensated for
their dependence on the towns with grudging disdain. The North
Grange on Friday afternoons was a raw edge, a badly carpentered
joint, where the bargain of existence was too plain. Here as usual
Journeyman was the hinge man, the middle worker.

Today would be different.

Since wrangling Peter Todbaum down the peninsula and into
his care, the Cordon people had looked at Journeyman with renewed curiosity. They waited for some revelation. Journeyman told
them only that Todbaum's car was parked. That the visitor had asked
nothing untoward, that he was presently welcome. If skeptical, the
Cordon people didn't press. That Eke and his unnamed friend had
absconded into the region of the towns went unmentioned. It was
possible that the Cordon had no idea where the two men had taken
themselves.

But, one week earlier, Journeyman had been helping a Cordon
woman named Carol Leeds load her horse, when she said, "The elders are hoping for a parley this time next week."

Carol Leeds was a forceful, sixtysomething Mainer with tattoos
that ran beyond her shirt-cuffs and across her knuckles, also up her

throat right to her jawline. A woman whose presence Journeyman found both intimidating and impressive, one who only rarely made the expedition to the North Grange.

Journeyman had only widened his eyes.

"Can you make it happen?" Carol Leeds had asked him.

"I think so."

She nodded. Journeyman was left to alert the towns. Of course, in their anarchistic fashion, there was no appointed authority to notify. The makeup of whatever diplomatic party might join Journeyman in meeting with the Cordon elders was sheerly a matter of whom he chose to alert. And whomever they chose to share it with.

Journeyman supposed he could even have decided to alert Todbaum. His storytelling and coffee had made Founder's Park as much a public commons as anything the towns had seen since the early days of the Arrest.

Journeyman did not alert Todbaum.

The day of the meeting the company consisted of Journeyman and Quentin as usual. Also Mike Raritan, who cooked out of the old roadside lobster shack and whose mackerel-and-potato fritters were something the towns had used from the start to beguile the Cordon. Dog treats, Journeyman had often thought, for the peninsula's guard dogs. Mike carried a basket of them to the parley. Versatile Paulo had come, their tree warden and piano tuner.

Spodosol had sent a representative: Cynthia Pitchings, a protégée of Seldon and Margot, a carrier of the old wisdom. Cynthia was bridge to the generation that had, under spell of the Stevedores' bestselling back-to-the-land manifesto, *Living the Real Life*, inaugurated the organic movement here, living in an atmosphere almost of voluntary Arrest. Astur had come along too, as Cynthia's second. Two men Journeyman barely knew, named Eugene and Paul, were here from Granite Head.

A pair of surprise attendees, too, from East Tinderwick. One of the mothers from the rarely glimpsed deep-woods families, Delia Limetree. She'd come with her son. He was the teenager, the strapping solitary twin who'd been in the park with Todbaum at the first story. Today Journeyman learned his name: Sterling. He seemed keyed up, his mother mournful. What had compelled them here? Sterling carried a knapsack.

On the Cordon's side, Carol Leeds, with two others of their elders, Cyrus and Deloit. The two wore long beards and biker leathers, and gear like fingerless gloves and flip-up shades to sing out their Road Warrior dreams for anyone who'd listen, but the eyes beneath the flip-ups were careworn, watery like poached eggs, as though they'd been weeping. Younger members had come too, a group of five men and women who didn't linger inside. They helped themselves to a fritter, or took some packets from the table to load, then stood out on the road talking in low tones.

One of the younger men was short a hand and forearm. The man moved the thick-wrapped elbow stump tentatively, gazing at it with an air of wonder, unlike the carelessness Journeyman associated with Vietnam and Gulf War veterans, street-corner presences gesticulating with decades-missing limbs. The last time Journeyman had seen this man he'd been whole, he was certain of it.

The three elders, Leeds, Cyrus, and Deloit, sat stiffly arranged at one of the Grange's family-style tables. Not reaching into the basket of fritters, though the younger folks had broken the seal. Those from the towns stood, or perched on chairs at the fringe. Journeyman gathered, reluctantly, that he was seen as the liaison. He flipped away the cloth covering the basket and handed the fritters around. The smell was good. The elders fell on them wolfishly. Paulo and Astur accepted them as well, in the cause of conviviality. They took Journeyman's hint, moving their chairs nearer to the long table. Paulo poured rose hip tea from a thermos into mugs from the Grange's ancient kitchen.

Sterling Limetree and his mother hung on the periphery for now.

"Guess I'll get straight to it," said Deloit. "You won't be surprised, concerns your man and his nuclear-engine car."

He's no one's man, Journeyman wanted to say. He moved around the table to place hot mugs in Eugene's and Paul's hands, drawing them into the circle. Journeyman said nothing, however. Let him be a fixture, an apparatus; let him not be taken for a spokesperson. "Your man had some friends," Deloit continued, "only I guess I don't mean friends. Came looking for him in numbers, about a month ago now, along the same road I came in on."

"Which road is that, actually?" asked Paulo.

Deloit, already suspicious of trickery, squinted. "Came across out of Rangeley, the Lakes, maybe White Mountains. Beyond our control."

"Not up from the cities?" Paulo meant up along the old 95 route, the ruined four-lane from Portland and beyond—Boston, maybe New York City too. Journeyman had heard it claimed that the Cordon themselves had wrecked the asphalt, to thwart or slow the approach of anything they lacked the firepower to repel. Ironically enough.

"If he did, he'd tacked well to the interior before getting near to us."

"The ones that followed him, have you tried talking to them?" This was Mike Raritan. Journeyman thought: We have a government. Paulo and Mike are our government. Today.

"It's not talking they're after." At this from Deloit, Journeyman felt them all glance through the Grange's window, which framed the young men and women on the steps outside, including that one staring from time to time at the bandage on his elbow and the space below it. Did the Cordon finally face more than a propped-up adversary? Be careful what you wish for, Journeyman thought.

"What are you here to propose?" asked Cynthia Pitchings. Now she was in their government too. Or always had been. She was a vestige of the old government, perhaps, that generation toughened in their disappointed-utopian skins.

"We'd like that machine now," said Deloit. "We could use it, I'm not too proud to say."

"You mean to turn it over to them?"

"Ma'am, speaking frankly, I mean to ram it down their throats."

"You think that's best?"

"Not to rupture your illusions, but there's those who can't be appeased with kind words and fish fritters, and that's what we're dealing with now. If you want to leave this work to us, and you do, then you'll have to take our word for it."

"You want us to send him *back*?"

That voice was Journeyman's—high, sudden, and completely startling. He hadn't meant to speak.

Outside, one of the horses snorted.

38.

WHAT DID JOURNEYMAN WANT?

WHAT DID JOURNEYMAN WANT? COULD he possibly want the Cordon to drag Todbaum away? Did he want to warn Todbaum?

Was Journeyman in a panic because he feared Todbaum couldn't defend himself, or because he feared that he would?

Did Journeyman dream of riding with Todbaum into battle in his impregnable, unlikely machine, the last real machine on planet Earth? If so, would it be alongside or *against* the Cordon from the south?

Did Journeyman simply want, despite his best interest, to see what would become of Founder's Park were Todbaum permitted to continue contriving whatever it was he was contriving there, his coffee klatch from hell?

Well, at least Journeyman was certain he didn't want the attention his outcry had gained him. He took the empty teapot to the Grange kitchen, then hung in the doorway beside Quentin, to try and make himself invisible. Feeling in his pocket for Todbaum's napkin contract, he discovered it had already been soaked in his palm's nervous sweat.

39.

A BIG MEETING, PART 2

DELOIT LEANED BACK, EYES HALF-SHUT, and smoothed his beard as though squeezing liquid from it. Cyrus was the one who answered Journeyman's question. "Nope. We've got no interest in your man. He's too much a hot potato, an enemy maker. We want the motherfucking thing turned over empty."

"What are you suggesting we do?" asked Mike Raritan.

Cyrus shrugged. "It's your problem. We never lay eyes on him again, it's a good thing."

"None of us knows how to drive it," said Mike.

"We all watched him. It wasn't brain surgery." Cyrus glanced at Journeyman where he stood, insufficiently hidden in the kitchen doorway. "Word from Eke was, Sandy got took for a little ride."

"Just once," Journeyman said.

"So, Sandy's the deliverer, let him deliver it. We got a good relationship."

"Eke and his friend," said Cynthia Pitchings. "They've been occupying the woods near Founder's Park. Is there some purpose in this we should understand?"

"We don't want violence," said Paulo.

Deloit showed his upper gums. "Sure, you got us for that."

"What are they doing?"

"You go ask them that yourselves. Eke and Walt didn't come on our behalf. They bugged out of their own accord. Maybe they got shy about killing. Just like you all."

The meeting had taken a turn, grown restive. Or maybe it was suddenly finished. At this moment Delia and Sterling Limetree made themselves known. The teenager vibrated on the brink of some outburst, it seemed to Journeyman. What grievance brought him here? Maybe he'd come as Todbaum's proxy in some way. Proxy, or dupe. It was his mother who finally spoke.

"I want a promise from one of you," she said. "I can't stop him from going, but I want someone to say they're looking out for him. He's not as old as he looks."

This made no sense: Sterling didn't look old at all. The boy stood forward, dropping his small pack at his feet. "I want to fight," he said.

Mike Raritan, Paulo, Astur, and Cynthia Pitchings, all on Journeyman's side of the gathering, only waited to understand. The Cordon elders showed no surprise.

"I'll watch your boy," said Carol Leeds evenly.

"See, this is *good*," said Deloit, suddenly jubilant. If he'd had a mug of ale in his hand, he'd have clapped it on the table for emphasis. "We need bodies, lean ones. We trade a couple of losers like your new forest friends, and we pick up a kid with some piss in him. Welcome aboard."

This had the flavor of a ritual occurrence. New to the towns, but a thing the Cordon might have enacted a hundred times. A script Journeyman might have rewritten but not put his name to.

"He's fifteen," said Delia Limetree.

"Eke might have been no more than fifteen, five years ago," said Deloit. "He was pretty good then, too. Better than he ended up. You're a twin, boy?"

"Yes, sir," said Sterling.

"Wouldn't mind a two for one. Seeing how we lost two."

"His brother isn't interested," said Delia.

"Just asking."

"Maybe it is time for us to finish this meeting," said Astur, speaking for the first time. "We have heard your request. Now we must consider what to do."

"Okeydoke," said Deloit.

"She's right," said Carol Leeds. When she opened her mouth, Deloit closed his. Was she the one truly in charge? "These people have a problem they need to work out," Leeds went on. "We'll wait for the results. Time to thank them for the food and ride home."

"And we'll be glad to care for the two men who have been dismissed from your protection," Astur continued, as though the ending of the meeting was suddenly hers to direct. "They'll need to work, of course. Everyone needs to make a contribution."

"Couldn't agree more, little lady," said Deloit. He swept up another fritter from the basket and stood. "Let's roll." He put his gloved hand on Sterling's shoulder and the boy seemed to cradle into Deloit's presence there. Deloit might practically have strapped Sterling to his voluminous chest and belly.

"*He's too young*," cried Delia Limetree. She stood alone ungrouped, in her own drama of parting. To whom did she petition? Carol Leeds? Maybe some unseen jury to judge them all. No such body existed.

The room lapsed into silence. The murmur of the younger Cordon people who'd stayed on the porch leaked in. Along with it, the breath and shifting of the tethered horses. The room in which they met was just an old box, clapboard and shingle slapped together in the nineteenth century by people long dead. Untended woods grew ever closer on all sides. If they remained silent long enough, they might even hear it growing.

Journeyman felt himself helplessly shredding Todbaum's world-altering napkin with all the strength in his fingers.

Into this stupefied wrongness came the most unexpected voice. "I'll go with him," said Quentin. He slid from behind Journeyman. His voice crabbed and whiny as ever. Yet Journeyman heard in it a kind of resolve. "I'll watch him for you." He spoke to Delia Limetree, and to Deloit. "Then you'll have two, two for your two lost."

"Right," said Deloit, as if he'd predicted this as well. "Okay. Welcome to the revolution."

40.

AFTERMATH OF A BIG MEETING

THEY LEFT, THEN, TAKING STERLING Limetree and Quentin with them. Quentin had only needed a moment to gather a small bag—or had he somehow had it prepared in advance? The peninsula group, smaller than before, was left to spill out into the sunshine, to dissolve itself, on an afternoon over which it felt a curtain should fall. None did. Paulo and Mike Raritan and Cynthia Pitchings had journeyed on Spodosol Farm's horses. They mounted and started back, Paulo making room for Delia Limetree on his horse. The two from Granite Head, Eugene and Paul, had horses too, but stood for a moment with Journeyman and Astur, watching the others depart.

Journeyman's sense of guilt was both sharp and obscure. Was it meant to be him, instead of Quentin, who'd gone with Sterling Limetree into the Cordon's ranks? I have a job, he wanted to protest aloud. I am the deliverer and the butcher's assistant. I am required at the Lake of Tiredness. But no one had accused him of shirking enlistment.

"They're crazy," Journeyman heard himself say. "I don't know how to drive the Blue Streak. No one does."

"Might be a lucky thing they want to take it off your hands," said Paul. Journeyman didn't know him well. He didn't know anyone from Granite Head well.

"I think it might require voice recognition to even start up," Journeyman said, trying to batten the rising note of panic in his voice. "What are they going to do, drag it to Belfast behind a team of stallions?"

Eugene grunted a laugh. "Pair of pullers might do the job, now that you mention it."

"Are they asking us to kill him?" Journeyman said. "Because that's what it sounds like to me."

"Listen, Mr. Duplessis." Paul spoke with a chilling flatness. Journeyman felt the distance between Granite Head and East Tinderwick. Granite Head had the luxury of deciding Todbaum wasn't their problem.

"Yes?"

Journeyman glanced quickly to find Astur. She'd gone to retrieve her bicycle, and his, from the shoulder where they stood tilted against a pair of birches. Paul kept his voice low. "We've been talking. Feeling is, we don't need some broad consensus this time round. The community's got no stake in any kind of restorative justice." The man from Granite Head used the term neutrally, without contempt. Journeyman recognized the comparison it was meant to evoke, even before Paul nailed it down: "He isn't one of our own, like Kormentz."

Restorative justice? Kormentz's so-called trial had been a disaster. After weeks of house arrest in his yurt behind Spodosol's orchard he'd been present for the ad hoc tribunals, at the start. Then was banished, for his unwillingness to shut up, for attempting to filibuster judgment off into the indefinite future. (Imagine Todbaum given a similar opportunity.) In the end, it had been one of the teenagers Kormentz molested who'd proposed that Kormentz should go to the cabin by the long north pond to be supervised and fed by the towns, rather than sent off to a likely death beyond their boundary. The girl coined the name on the spot: *send him to the Lake of Tiredness*. It might have been her judgment on them all.

"What's he accused of, anyway?" Journeyman asked now. Astur approached, guiding both bicycles by the stems. Journeyman doubted he could have managed such an elegant trick.

"It isn't what he's accused of, it's what he's brought down on us. What he's capable of. Look at how he's got the Cordon riled. Left a trail of people riled before he got to the Cordon, it looks like. Him and his machine have got to go, together or apart."

"I'm open to suggestions as to how," said Journeyman.

"Nope. This one's on you. You and your sister." Paul glanced, again, at Astur. She smiled. No way to know what she'd heard.

Eugene and Paul took themselves away on their horses, leaving Journeyman with Astur. The meeting was over, unless he and Astur constituted a meeting. He'd mounted his bicycle before realizing the North Grange needed shuttering, with Quentin gone. They went inside, cleared the dishes to the kitchen. Journeyman wondered if some other stray person would set up here, at their perimeter, or if the structure would remain empty. He felt heavy with loss. First, loss of the two neighbors who'd made the insane crossing-over into the Cordon. A special loss, too, a dent in the geometry of the towns. From now on, Journeyman considered, he'd have to open the Grange himself for the transfer of goods.

He bicycled with Astur down the road. No horses in sight, nothing but crows and a string of turkeys who funky-chickened grudgingly from their path. The sun was low. They navigated the frost heaves. Journeyman protected his newly repaired wheel.

"What are we going to do?" All he could do not to ask, *What does Maddy want to do?* But Maddy had recused herself, as she'd declined to attend this meeting. Astur wasn't his sister's proxy, even if Paul's glance had suggested he thought so.

Maddy might restrict herself to midnight visits, to hammer and tongs, or hand-hewn explosives like those once employed by the Unabomber.

"It's a very interesting question!" said Astur.

"Well, yes."

"The two young men will really have to be put to some use," she said. "I've been thinking to send them to Quarry Island."

"Quarry Island?"

"Yes. It's time to begin work on the lighthouse for real. Though they'll first have to build themselves some shelter for the winter."

Had she misunderstood Journeyman's question? Or chosen to ignore it? At times, Astur made Journeyman feel as if Todbaum were his, Journeyman's, figment—a thing only Journeyman could see.

They stopped their bicycles at the juncture where Astur would turn off toward East Tinderwick.

"Astur, may I ask a question?"

"Of course."

"Does Maddy have—" Journeyman started again. "Will Maddy go to the park?" She'd already been to the park—Astur must have known this.

"I think it is an excellent question."

"Todbaum's kind of . . . fixated."

"I'm more struck by the way so many fixate on him."

"I have something—" Attempting to deliver the napkin from his pocket into Astur's care, Journeyman rained shreds onto the ground. Journeyman's palm was stained with sweated-off ink, blurred impressions of the nonsense Todbaum had written there. Astur watched him curiously. The napkin blew away, tatters on the road.

"Would you like to join for dinner, Sandy?" she said. "I'm sure we could discuss it further."

"Oh, thanks, but not tonight."

"Plans?"

"I'm supposed to visit a . . . friend." Journeyman felt humiliated. He didn't know her name yet. The woman in the library hardly expected him—the only scheme in which he was "supposed" to do anything besides wallow in his lonely rooms was that in his inconsolable skull.

41.

HIS LONELY ROOMS

FOUR ROOMS, ABOVE WHAT HAD once been the florist and candy shop. Bed, bath, ill-used kitchen, front room with dormer alcove and a sliver of bay view—though sight of Quarry Island was occluded from here by the spit of land between the Tinderwicks. On the daybed of the alcove, books rustled from the library before the new arrival's occupation there. Most arranged in a neat row and dusty with good intentions, Graeber's *Debt*, Gibbon's *Decline and Fall*, the Stevedores' *Living the Real Life*, Pynchon's *Gravity's Rainbow*, Eliot's *Middlemarch*. Open to the cushion on its face, a paperback of Ross Thomas's *The Fools in Town Are on Our Side*.

Elsewhere, not much. On the kitchen table, a squeezed-out tube of Needra's homemade toothpaste, overdue for return and refilling. Shoved in a kitchen cabinet, a dead laptop full of scripts and treatments, QuickTime files of personal erotica, etc., etc. Closet floor, a pistol in a shoebox, equally useless, equally forgotten. Journeyman never imagined he'd actually use it anyway.

No mirrors.

Journeyman was elsewhere: bolstering his courage to knock on the door of the library.

42.

DRENKA

"MAY I COME IN?"

"If there's a book you want, just tell me and I'll find it." She addressed him through the partly open door. Her dark hair was cut short, and in a somewhat irregular shape—she'd been cutting it herself, he supposed. Her gaze was steady and bright and possibly amused. It was true that the woman in the library had found Sei Shōnagon's *Pillow Book* for him, weeks before, demonstrating her aptitude in the stacks. Still, it was the library. This wasn't her most appealing trait.

"People sometimes like to browse." Not the footing on which Journeyman had hoped to start.

"Is that what you want? To browse?"

He wondered if they'd ever manage to have a conversation besides this one. "I didn't mean to surprise you. It isn't really about a book."

She only blinked, unwilling to help him.

"Do you want to go for a walk?"

"Wait," she said, and closed the door. Journeyman was returned to himself, to the scouring bankruptcy of the late afternoon. He felt empty-handed with nothing to deliver. That had been the point: to appear here as other-than-the-deliveryman. Yet what was he?

When she slipped through the door to join him she wore a sweatshirt with the hood drawn up. Perhaps she'd noticed him inspecting her haircut. Or was cold. The sun edged at the horizon; it was reasonable to be cold.

They meandered together toward the water, through the parking area of the abandoned hospital. Though it continued to be a fund of supplies and equipment, the sick and dying preferred to be tended nearly anywhere but in the vast empty facility.

"Will you tell me your name now?"

"Drenka."

"I'm Alexander," he said. "I think I told you before." Then admitted, "Mostly called Sandy."

"It fits you," she said, crushingly.

All Journeyman's possible questions seemed inane. The one he selected—"What brings you?"—Drenka preempted, raising her hand.

"I don't want to be interrogated."

"I'm not here representing anyone but myself."

"Then I don't want to be interrogated by *you*."

"What should we talk about?"

"Tell me about your day, Alexander Duplessis. Who did you see?"

"You don't know them, I think—"

"Explain it to me. Tell me a story."

A story? That was what Journeyman was meant for. Or had been, once. "You know how there's this perimeter around us here? Those people call themselves the Cordon—" Journeyman hesitated: Was this even true? Or had the people in the towns arrived at that name? "We had a meeting with them today."

Drenka waved as if brushing this off. "I avoided all that. I came by water."

"I didn't ask."

"What do you mean?"

"You're self-interrogating now, I just want to point out."

"You were saying."

"So the Cordon, they're a little stirred up. Normally no one comes or goes. They, uh, let this guy through—" Where to start with Todbaum? Journeyman didn't want to, actually.

"The car guy?"

"You heard?"

"People come around," she said. "You know, the ones you mentioned. Those who like to browse."

"Well, yes. The car guy. He set some stuff in motion."

"He wasn't as discreet as me."

"Not so discreet." Journeyman couldn't be more ambivalent about the topic. Though he felt cheered by the jostling, elbowy shape his and Drenka's talk had begun to take. "Some of their people are living with us, and today a couple of our people crossed over . . ."

"You seem unnerved."

"I do?" How to explain what it meant to have Sterling Limetree and Quentin Maslow go? Minor characters, he couldn't think how to make them matter to Drenka. Had Todbaum been giving Journeyman notes on a script, he'd have instructed Journeyman to cut the two out entirely. Yet a part of Journeyman had gone with them. He and Drenka walked in silence, to the water.

"Sandy."

"Yes?" Journeyman didn't, just then, like the sound of his nickname in her mouth. Better her mocking him with the full string of syllables.

"Thanks for the company. I'm going to walk on alone now."

He blinked at her dumbly.

"If you want to browse in the library, you can do that now."

"It's okay."

"I'll see you again soon." She shook his hand. He watched her pick her way along the rock beach, into the chill wind.

How did one human undesolate another? If you'd never seen it done, you wouldn't believe it possible.

As for stories, they might be among the kind of machines that no longer worked.

43.

DINNER WITH JANE AND LUCIUS

JANE AND LUCIUS, THE MARIJUANA cultivators, were occasional guests at the Farm. Journeyman couldn't tell what triggered the invitations. Once or twice a season they trotted in with a basket containing bottles of wine from their apparently inexhaustible cellar and something interesting from Lucius's kitchen. Spodosol was changed on those nights, in unquantifiable ways. It wasn't as though pot, or alcohol, weren't present at other times. But Jane and Lucius seemed a cue to drop the usual atmosphere of conscientious industry in favor of something more unbuttoned. When they came, evenings ended late.

The two lived outside East Tinderwick, in a compound of summer houses that had been occupied for just three or four weeks a summer by wealthy Boston families and a famous painter, though they were not summer people. They carried a certain cosmopolitan air. Lucius had been, once, the chef at the Tinderwick Inn. That was before the Arrest made such things as inns and restaurants irrelevant, and the inn a permanent home for the resident staff and a couple of guests who'd happened to be checked in.

Journeyman was envious of them. With Journeyman, Maddy

was all work and no play. When Jane and Lucius appeared, she'd abandon a row of kohlrabi half-tended and drink wine in daylight. This night Lucius placed a superb cassoulet at Maddy and Astur's table, made from a duck Journeyman had dressed himself. The room was ringed with candles, a circle of light pushing against the darkening October. They'd shared an early smoke and were through the salad course before the subject arose.

"I could go for one of those espressos of his right now," said Lucius. He'd unbuttoned his vest and leaned back in his chair. Journeyman had no idea when Lucius and Jane might have visited the new Founder's Park. He wasn't surprised they had.

"Go and have one if you like," said Astur.

"The price is too high," Lucius quipped.

"That guy's a major *douche*," said Jane, which brought a sharp snort of laughter from Journeyman. "His whole Catastrophe Svengali routine is a fucking drag. It's like he thinks he invented the end of the world."

Lucius made a wry face. "Still, Jane. You can't say the guy didn't do his homework." Jane and Lucius made a specialty of this affectionate push-pull banter, while others were usually too ripped on their weed to be able to form sentences. It was a style of sociality Journeyman missed more than he realized.

"What's that supposed to mean?"

"While we were huddled up here in Podunk, the man drove the length of the goddamn country, babe. No wonder he's pulling a crowd. Inquiring minds want to know."

"I call horseshit," said Jane. "Who *knows* where he came from?"

"Well, Sandy does. Don't you, Sandy?"

"I knew him in L.A.," Journeyman admitted. "Actually before that, in college."

"What do you mean *knew* him?" said Jane. "You know him now."

"Or is he not the same guy?" said Lucius, holding up a finger, playing Sherlock Holmes. "Maybe we've got some doubts?"

"I wish I could claim he was an impersonator," Journeyman said. "Or that he's changed." He avoided Maddy's eye, now. No reason to imagine anyone knew about the Starlet Apartments, unless it was Astur. He avoided her eye too. They made it easy for him, rising together to clear the plates, into the kitchen. But they were hardly out of earshot.

"Okay, so he's a producer, right?" Lucius spoke as a prosecuting attorney, nailing down established facts. "The thing about producers is that they're producing something, usually several things at once."

"He's a *liar*," said Jane.

"Same thing," said Lucius. "So, what's he producing? He's gonna make a little Cordon of his own, right?"

"Out of *what*? Or I mean *who*? Ted Nowlin? They already stole his teenager."

"That was a trade," Journeyman pointed out. "He swapped the teenager for the men in the woods. Eke and his friend. Walt." Journeyman had told no one what he'd seen.

"Out of us, babe. We're all gonna be in it, just you wait."

"You're making no fucking sense," said Jane.

"He won't have use of Eke and Walt," said Astur, who'd returned from the kitchen with a serving bowl of preserved berries and goat cheese. "I've enlisted them in my project. They're going to live on Quarry Island."

"That so?" asked Lucius, with amusement. "Have Rosencrantz and Guildenstern been informed of their place in your plans?"

Astur's smile was placid. "They're making themselves ready for their departure from the mainland. Camping in the park is excellent practice."

But Jane wasn't going to be put off. "Say what you mean, Luce. How are we going to be in his Cordon?"

Lucius shut his eyes, as if explaining might be beneath his dignity. "Listen, when they come for him, and they *are* going to come for him, what are we going to end up doing?" No one answered. "That's right, we'll fight to protect him and his fucking artisanal panzer. We gave that jackass asylum, didn't we? We more or less offered him amnesty too, for whatever atrocities he committed on their turf. He's one of us now. If we let them pull him out, what's next?" Lucius widened his arms dramatically, and bugged his eyes. "This. All this shit. They take it all."

"He's not one of us," said Jane.

"He is, Jane. He's us all the way. He's our spirit animal. He bought us for an espresso."

"Oh, that's utter horseshit, Luce. You're drunk."

"Sure. I'm blitzed and it's working on me like a truth serum."

"Maybe *you'll* be fighting for him," said Jane. Her contempt was royal. "I'll be sitting in the peanut gallery, watching through opera glasses, laughing my big fat lily-white ass off."

All laughed. Maddy laughed loudest. They'd all turned to her, aware she'd spoken the least through the dinner—spoken barely at all. Yet she presided. They were here at her pleasure, weren't they? Journeyman considered it, his ritual puzzle. The survival of the peninsula was at her pleasure—or hers and Astur's and that of five or six of the other most expert farmers. The farmers and Victoria—the Cordon loved Victoria's sausage.

But Journeyman had fallen silent too. Pretending he was invisible, undeputized. "Will you go and see him, Maddy?" he blurted now.

"I'm not as curious as the rest of you."

"I don't mean because you're curious. Todbaum thinks this is between you and him."

"He's wrong." Through the revels Maddy had never unholstered her hammer. It hung from her belt casually, a piece of her. The same hammer she'd used to stress-test Peter Todbaum's cockpit.

"Wrong because he's crazy—" Journeyman began this as a question, but it hung as an assertion.

"We're all fucking officially crazy," said Lucius, who was, it seemed to Journeyman, fucking officially drunk.

"Wrong because he's got the wrong sibling," said Maddy, as she got up to clear the dishes.

44.

POSTAPOCALYPTIC AND DYSTOPIAN STORIES

IF JOURNEYMAN WAS AN EXPERT in one thing, it was post-apocalyptic and dystopian stories. Reading them, to pillage riffs and motifs for *Yet Another World*, had been his paid homework for decades, in the time before the Arrest. Paid by Todbaum, that's to say. Todbaum hadn't only been outsourcing his research, however. He read the books too.

"You know what's great about this shit, don't you?" he'd once asked Journeyman.

They sat in his Venice Boulevard office, headquarters of his production company, Kill Tree, control room for the vehicle he piloted before the Blue Streak. With the question, he'd gestured at the books strewn everywhere, pages stuffed with Post-its and striped by hot-pink and canary highlighters, many laid open on their faces. More than once Journeyman had witnessed Todbaum physically hacking a chapter from the bindings, to place in the hands of Journeyman or some other alphabet-monkey he'd hired to adapt the stolen material into a scene. The strange thing, the very most Todbaumest thing, was that he always insisted his assistant buy first editions for his raw material. The best copies, dust jackets intact. Then he'd slough off the jackets to be trampled. He'd say he liked the smell and feel of the original editions. Yet once acquired they were doomed. (Journeyman had once reached to shift *Cat's Cradle* from an oozing pool of spilled cola. Todbaum laughed sharply. "Look at you, Sandman. You feel sorry for the *books*, don't you?")

That day Journeyman had come to report on Walter Tevis's *Mockingbird*. Journeyman said he didn't think it was a movie. Todbaum only grunted. Very likely this hadn't been his hope. More, he wanted to load Journeyman's mind with examples to pillage for *Yet Another World*. Tevis's book, *Earth Abides*, *Dr. Bloodmoney*, *Station Eleven*, *A Canticle for Leibowitz*, *Riddley Walker*, Vonnegut, Atwood, King—these, sprawled around them, were the *shit* he had in mind.

"What's so great about this shit?" Journeyman parroted.

"It's always better, not worse."

"What do you mean?"

"You people are supposed to, you know, write it to *keep* it from happening, right? Cautionary tales?" In Todbaum's mind Journeyman might be answerable for all writers, his tribe. "But they just can't help it, they like it there. They *love* it there."

"Where?"

"Where? Whatever fucked-up allegorical hellscape or dire prison block for the human soul they're working through, the particulars don't matter. They want to live there, you can feel it. The characters in the book, they're always justified, set on a road. Speaking of which, *The Road*, that one bugs the fuck out of me. It's supposed to be this existential Beckett deal, right? Grown-up apocalypse. But what's the worst old Cormac can think of? The basement scene, right? They keep those people alive so they can strip the flesh off them to eat. But the thing no one ever mentions? You'd have to feed those people to keep 'em alive. There's no point to it. If McCarthy were honest, he'd admit he wrote a campfire story, Sandman. Instead he inserts all this Old Testament horseshit. The world's reduced and cleansed, the ambiguity scrubbed out."

"Because—it's easier?"

"Sure. Postapocalyptic comfort food. I'm not talking about dime-store fiction. Even Kafka wanted to go live in *The Castle*, I bet you good money."

"We tell ourselves stories in order to live."

"Sure. Who doesn't like *comfort*? And who doesn't like *food*?"

"Not me."

"There you go, Sandman. There you go. Now write my show just like that. A postapocalyptic, dystopian-pastoral meet-cute. The old song we all long to hear."

45.

WHAT DID THE
BLUE STREAK WANT?

JOURNEYMAN WOKE ON THE COUCH downstairs. Not because
Maddy and Astur's guest room, his usual crash pad at Spodosol,
wasn't available, but because he'd passed out on the couch after
bullshitting with Jane and Lucius long into the night. They'd broken into a supply of hard cider after exhausting Jane and Lucius's
red wine, and the conversation turned foul and foolish. By the time
it was just the three of them, there was less and less Journeyman
remembered.

Journeyman discovered Maddy and Astur already gone, presumably to their morning labors. The kitchen woodstove was lit. He
found a still-warm pot of tea waiting, with a mug set out. They'd
tiptoed around him. He sat and sipped and blinked in the slanted
morning light and waited for his head to clear. He'd dreamed of Todbaum, of the old days, of the talk concerning dystopian and postapocalyptic stories. Maybe it was all dreamed, maybe there had never
been a Todbaum, or a Hollywood, no life before. No. It had happened, then been muddled into dream. Journeyman missed it.

Once he felt steady enough to balance on his bicycle, Journeyman started out, not searching the greenhouses to find his sister,

not wanting to face her in his morning-after incarnation. He should have returned to Tinderwick, to his duties. Instead he veered into Founder's Park. If he ever wanted Todbaum to himself, it should be early. By midafternoon Todbaum usually had some audience of visitors or acolytes around him.

Journeyman could ask for a coffee. He needed one.

The park was quiet, the fire dark, the Blue Streak silent. Far across the water he saw a sail, off the east of Quarry Island. No signs of life beyond the tree line, where Eke and Walt kept their tent. Journeyman leaned his bicycle against the playground slide and approached the machine. The ladder was retracted. Nothing indicated life or activity within. Perhaps Todbaum was still asleep. At the moment of this thought, Journeyman heard a summoning whistle from the water's edge, past the gazebo.

"Sandy, hey. Hang on a sec."

Todbaum stood just below sight line on the embankment, peeing into the bushes. He shook off and zipped, then jogged in his slovenly way up to join Journeyman. His jeans were almost black with filth, his sneakers soaked in dew. The smile that played on his face was sickly. This was the farthest Journeyman had ever caught him from his machine. Journeyman stood between them. He could tackle Todbaum into the grass, then seize—but no.

The harsh light of morning, the harsh light of Journeyman's hangover, these flooded the scene, seeming to strip it of illusion. Todbaum looked terribly old. Journeyman had been Time Averaging him relentlessly since his return. It was as though Todbaum's charismatic sway over the visitors to his storyteller's circle formed a kind of gauze, a liquid aura, which enclosed and recuperated Todbaum himself. Now, bare of it, he only appeared anemic, insalubrious, deranged by time. Journeyman might have looked the same to Todbaum.

"You only love me for my coffee."

"I wouldn't say no," Journeyman admitted.

"That's the spirit." As Todbaum passed him, Journeyman heard the Blue Streak stir, an almost subterranean sound of coolant rumbling, the silenced engines purring into life. Looking up, Journeyman saw the cockpit now glowed in readiness. The ladder rungs appeared. Had it sensed Todbaum's approach? Did Todbaum carry what used to be called a "key-chain fob"? If Journeyman intended either to help overthrow or to defend Todbaum, this might be important to know.

"C'mon up." Journeyman watched Todbaum's ass wriggle through the aperture, followed by his wet sneakers. Journeyman followed.

Inside, Todbaum pointed through the dome, to the lawn between the supercar's left side and the tree line. At first Journeyman imagined Todbaum had meant to indicate something in the woods—Eke and Walt's campsite, most likely. No. Todbaum pointed down, at the grass.

"You see the deer?"

Journeyman hadn't, until now. A younger buck, with a six- or eight-point rack, lay below, dead. The creature's carcass straddled a margin where the green lawn met singed-brown grass ringing the Blue Streak. Had the vehicle, to supply itself, drained the moisture and vitality from the nearest growth? Several pipes and tubes now extended from the underside of its chassis, into the ground. Or was this dead zone a result of the steady leakage of its radiation, as Journeyman had feared? And what about the deer? Journeyman asked this, and Todbaum smirked.

"It happened last night, I didn't hear a thing. Sometimes the Streak defends itself against threats."

"How's that a threat?"

"Idiot thing might've been clattering its hooves on my valves, who knows. Maybe it mistook us for a mating rival and tried to pick an antler fight."

My valves, mistook *us*, defends *itself*. At times Todbaum spoke of the supercar as if it were his own body. Other times, as if it were a phenomenon alien to him. Perhaps he was as confused as Journeyman. The Cordon, in proposing the townspeople separate him from it, had made Journeyman see Todbaum and the Blue Streak as separable. Yet Journeyman had supposed Todbaum was the car's master. What if the reverse were true?

"So, what's the wake-up call about, Sandy? You here to read me the riot act?"

"I crashed at Maddy's last night," Journeyman said, semi-apologetically. Semi-apology being perhaps his life mode supreme.

"You give her the contract?"

"Yes," Journeyman lied. "She's thinking it over."

"Game on," said Todbaum. "This is gonna be epic, when me and her get together."

"Peter, you know, don't you—she's a lesbian."

"Who isn't?"

At least a hundred reasons Journeyman could think of to ignore this remark. "There's something else."

"Then cut the circumlocution, baby. Eschew surplusage."

"I need to know what happened between you and the Cordon people."

"Why, exactly?"

"They see me as your—" Journeyman couldn't find this word, so he turned the phrase around. "They see you as my responsibility." He left the pronoun *they* unparticular. Let Todbaum think it meant only the Cordon, not the riders up from Granite Head. Not Maddy.

"So, you want me to tell you a story, huh?"

"Yes."

"Like a private viewing in a gallery, off-hours. Only I've got obligations to my regular audience now, Sandy. I can't waste the material."

"I don't want your *material*," Journeyman said. "I want the truth."

"What if the truth, my dear Alphonse, is that I plowed my treads over the skulls of a bunch of those fuckers? There might not be much more to it than that."

"I'd like to know the details."

"Well, you can wait. Where's your vaunted story sense? Can't you see the geographical arc of what I'm doing here, grinding across the vast terrain, the frontier thesis in reverse? Come back tonight, I'm doing Pennsylvania and New Jersey, into New York."

"I missed some chapters, I guess."

"Ninety percent of life is just showing up, Sanderton."

"I'll try to improve my attendance." Their banter felt perfunctory and empty, dress rehearsal for a show that had closed years before. Journeyman glanced at the dead deer. He wanted out of the cockpit, out of the grip of the lightly humming, radiation-leaking device that had magicked Peter Todbaum across the continent and back into his life. Journeyman considered its night luminosity, the strange fluorescence that lasted after the campfire died and the moon vacated, like a child's glow-in-the-dark pajamas. The glow made no sense for a crypto-military vehicle that might depend sometimes on stealth. Was the machine breaking down?

Seated in his swiveling pilot's chair, slurping espresso, Todbaum looked swallowed in decrepitude, barely animate. Perhaps the Blue Streak was a kind of life-support mechanism, operating Todbaum as its human proxy. What if it was ready to discard its meat puppet? *What did the Blue Streak want?*

Todbaum read his mind. "You're thinking I look like shit."

"Yes."

"Well, the feeling is mutual. You deserve to see this, coming around so early in the a.m. I don't feel human until the sun gets hot. Maybe three, four in the afternoon."

Feel human? Journeyman wanted to ask. How would you necessarily know?

"I'll come back tonight," he said to Todbaum. "I'll come back for the story."

46.

SPECIAL RIDER

"SHE WAS ANOTHER LIKE ME—maybe the first I'd met the whole way across. By that I mean she wasn't content to settle in one locality; she had ants in her pants. That isn't meant as a knock on you guys. What happened here is a general condition, the way of the world. But she just wasn't Arrested like everybody else. That got my attention right away. I guess you might say she was a *very arresting woman.*"

The fire lit the scene, lit the faces of Todbaum's regulars scattered around it. The widowers, Theodore Nowlin and Edwin Gorse. Sophie Thurber, that enigma. Mike Raritan now regularly came to take in the Todbaum stories, on what basis Journeyman couldn't know. Two women from Granite Head, Sarah and Eden, who'd come on bicycles, not for the first time. The teenagers, who hung at the gazebo as though on a street corner. Their contingent had grown. It seemed to Journeyman it might be half of those high school age. One of these was Danny Limetree, Sterling's bereft twin. The other teens had girded themselves around him, as though he'd become their wounded prince. A couple of off-the-gridders, names unknown to Journeyman, deep-woods hippies, him with dreadlocks, her in a turban and poncho, sat together. Andy, the town shrink—another surprise.

And Journeyman. He was a regular here, he supposed. The story underway concerned Todbaum's exit from Pittsburgh. He drew the scene unappealingly, as a region of militarized checkpoints, refugee camps, and bureaucratized resource distribution centers, like a permanent hurricane- or flood-management sector.

"I snuck my ass into this abandoned mall on the outskirts, a real negative zone. You remember what they called *ruin porn*? Well, I was living on set. Having rolled in with a couple weeks' supply of this and that I figured I could do some recon before I got too near to the East Coast, you know, the old enclaves, the Acela corridor. I wondered what anyone would: was there a teenage president, were the Nazis in charge, what did they replace the Empire State Building with, can you still get a good egg cream, did the Sox win the pennant, all that shit. But seriously, don't hold your breath because I have no fucking clue."

Creeping around the wings of this stage, Eke and Walt. They'd placed themselves in charge of the firewood. One or the other plunged in at intervals, almost gamboling, to add fuel to the blaze. It made an outlet for their nervy energy, perhaps also an excuse to be present without openly joining Todbaum's crowd. The former Cordon men now seemed to Journeyman to be holy innocents. Did they have an inkling of their place in Astur's scheme? Out across the water, Quarry Island revealed itself as a nullity, a blot where no starlight danced on the rippling water. It would have been on a night like this one that the French boat had grounded itself to pieces on the island's sea-facing rocks.

"It was the nearest thing to my current residency in your park, if you see it from a certain point of view. Not that I had anything to compare with you folks, shit. A few curious vagabonds came around to yak and bring me some examples of the local provender, but this was pretty abject stuff, goat's-head soup with dog-biscuit crackers on the side, that sort of thing. Nobody fetched me piping-hot corn-bread and rhubarb compote out in that neck of the woods."

Journeyman wondered not whether there was a teenage president, but who in the towns had gifted Todbaum with cornbread and compote.

"She turned up with her bag packed. Call it confidence or desperation, adds up to the same thing. Bag packed and a warning: they were about to move on me, to attack with a bunch of fertilizer explosives, a shit-bomb. Like your friends figured out, shit-tech might be the only tech that never gets Arrested. Only tech, honestly, that gives me the willies. So, she snuck up with her satchel in hand, a stolen loaf of pretty fair pumpernickel, and her one request: that I convey her down the road a patch, as they say. My first hitchhiker. What can I say? I'd gotten lonely by that point. I dug her chutzpah. I named this lady 'Pittsburgh,' just to needle her, since the only thing she'd tell me about herself was that she *wasn't* from around there."

Wonder, wonder, such things to wonder over. How had it all come to exactly *this*? When would Journeyman figure it out, if not now? Here in the oasis of time at the end of the world? Yet since Todbaum's arrival, time had perhaps restarted. Todbaum was his own ticking clock; he carried deadlines, crises. Worse than a clock. A ticking bomb.

Wonder this: If shit-tech was the only tech to outlast the Arrest, then what powered the Blue Streak? Was its fuel rod definable as a form of shit? Perhaps that was what separated Todbaum from most men: His turds could kill, his shit had kilowattage. His, far from being biodegradable and soil-nutritive, had a carcinogenic half-life.

"A little voice told me to take Pittsburgh's warning to heart. Same voice that had kept me alive to that point. Anyway, that mall wasn't a going concern, there was doodley-squat for me there. So, off we took. Pittsburgh turned out to be a weird bird. Hot and cold conversational-wise, though I did pry out of her—the night we drained the last of the Macallan—that she'd passed through the

Arrest's first phase in a desert arts colony in Taos, New Mexico. Poetry, she told me. I figured that was what she kept scribbling in the little blue notebook stashed in her bag. And, you'll pardon my French, but Pittsburgh was a hell of a cocktease, too. You know how when you used to flip cable channels at two a.m. it felt like you were *always about to see a bare tit*, only you never actually did? That was Pittsburgh all over. She had some kind of geisha-ninja superpower for dressing and undressing in layers. Always these furshlugginer layers. Being around her was worse than being alone, because alone I could do what I liked, alone I could at least dream."

Todbaum's stories, his ceaseless renditions of *that old song we long to hear*, where did it all come from? Could it be the first time Journeyman wondered this? He'd lived in Todbaum's verbal sewage flow for more than half his life. Todbaum wasn't simply a liar—he couldn't be *simply* anything. His tongue seemed wired to some invisible current: what his audience needed and feared to have spoken. Should Journeyman halt the tale and warn his listeners, the swelling constituency at Founder's Park, not to believe? He couldn't. He was part of the constituency. He'd come wishing to hear the truth beneath the lies, or beneath the stories, the mad pastiche—a recombinant hash of truth and untruth, of exaggeration and invention and translation, of sleight of hand, of this switched for that. The lie that tells the truth.

Todbaum's was a gross art. Journeyman craved it. It had something to tell him, he felt certain.

No doubt, that feeling in Journeyman was what Todbaum relied upon.

"She said she had friends in New York, that I should come with her there. I asked how she knew they were alive, or what made her think the city was in any shape to access, Manhattan not some walled-off maximum security island, or just long since starved into desolation, its hordes having skeletonized Dean & DeLuca and Gristedes within the first weeks. It ran against every instinct in my body to steer the Streak into the greater metropolitan area—I told her so. My notion was I'd swing north, cross the Hudson, get into the clear. But she had this sway with me, I can't say why. Like she'd really heard some long-distance call. Convinced me at least to drop her off in North Jersey, Hoboken maybe, near enough to see the skyline."

It seemed to Journeyman that the stories were growing meaner. Or perhaps just this one, specially cultivated for his command reception. Someone passed a flagon of hot mulled cider into Journeyman's hands. He took it gratefully, gulped a mouthful, and recoiled: it had been spiked with something as astringent as rubbing alcohol, or formaldehyde. A creature flapped in the trees overhead. Larger, Journeyman thought, than a crow. A raptor, maybe, sizing them, monitoring for strays from the flock.

"Turned out I cut her loose a few days too late. I had to kick the bitch to the curb. Finally snuck a look at her secret notebook. It wasn't poems. She'd been copying down every move I made, navigationally speaking, drawing up cute little diagrams of the dashboard and gauges, too, drafting up a proper little cookbook for mutiny."

Was this a warning? Did Todbaum know Journeyman had been charged, at least in the minds of the men from Granite Head, with dividing Todbaum from his machine? Journeyman had been only the Streak's second hitchhiker, after Pittsburgh. Todbaum had told him so. Yet it felt less the case than that Todbaum sought to get a rise from his listeners. As though he'd grown disgusted at how raptly they'd follow him anywhere. He wanted to toss it in their faces.

"That diva never put out, you know that? Instead she had me eating out of the palm of her hand, getting all in my cups, spilling my guts. Bitch never put out, not once. I should have ground her under my treads, smashed her in with me hobnail boot, the ungrateful cunt. All right, I've had enough of this crap for tonight, everybody go home."

47.

GORSE

JOURNEYMAN RAN INTO EDWIN GORSE the next day, a rare sighting on the main road. Gorse was agitated. He spoke with an air of implication, as though he and Journeyman had incurred a deep complicity the night before, at Founder's Park. This was out of character, in the extreme.

"We're going to need to mobilize our resources," he fretted. "This thing will test us in ways we haven't remotely prepared for."

"What thing, exactly?"

Gorse ignored the question. Though winter's extremes had flattened out, this was a true autumn afternoon, orange three-o'clockish light tilted off the bay waters visible between the library and town hall, leaves tumbleweeding down the empty street. "I've been talking with Theodore Nowlin," said Gorse. "He's with me, totally. It's time for those among us with organizational aptitudes to step to the fore. We can't just hope to stay viable as this sort of Tinkertoy community. I mean we'd better invest in our own values or admit they were always held at a very shallow level to begin with."

"I don't actually know how one invests in values," Journeyman hedged. The word made him wonder whether Gorse had been offended by Todbaum's drift the night before. By "cunt" and "bitch." But that wasn't it.

"By *defending* them," Gorse said angrily.

"Defending them how?" Journeyman said. "You mean by, like, protecting what's going on down at Founder's Park?"

"Why should that strike you as funny? The whole peninsula's a burning platform, Mr. Duplessis. But crisis also provides opportunity."

"No, I'm sure you're right. I just thought the Blue Streak was better able to defend itself than we are. Isn't that the whole point?"

"I suppose you'd rather not consider how we put ourselves in such a vulnerable position. Todbaum's come here to tell us who we are, and it isn't pretty."

"I suppose I'm with you there."

"You say that. But have you even listened to his accounts? The things he's seen?"

"I'm pretty sure that among the things he's seen is John Carpenter's *Escape from New York*," Journeyman said. "In fact, he used to have a production still of Adrienne Barbeau standing on the hood of a car holding a pistol taped up in his dorm room." Was Todbaum actually credible to someone like Gorse?

Journeyman at least felt he'd seen into Gorse, at last. The widower wasn't shy, he was angry. He'd come to the peninsula imagining his worldly successes would make him impressive, and no one had even noticed. Todbaum's arrival had reminded Gorse to remind others he was a necessary and serious person.

Journeyman thought of the motherless daughters, Gorse's captive audience. Was Gorse grooming their organizational aptitudes? Perhaps he was making his girls ready for the world he wished to see return. Journeyman wondered how many others wished for the same—not many, he suspected. He wasn't even certain that he did.

Gorse had hitched his star to Todbaum! Well, he was hardly the first.

48.

ON ASTUR'S BOAT AGAIN

JOURNEYMAN WAS REGULARLY ON ASTUR'S boat again. He thought very little of it—the old boatsickness had fled his body. He'd sail alone or with his sister, or with some others who relied on Astur for crossing back and forth to Quarry Island. Journeyman could finish his rounds by lunch, even on days when he had to visit the Lake of Tiredness. After that hour, he became Astur's boat boy, even learned a knot or two.

He was with her the day she ferried Eke and Walt across, with their tent, and stash of goods, and two extra backpacks loaded with dry goods and jars of preserved food, all organized for them by the Spodosolians. It came as a shock to see the two men all in readiness at the docks.

Journeyman exchanged names with Walt for the first time, before they entered the close quarters of Astur's sailboat. The two had grown hairier in their time in the woods. They smelled of the deep underbrush, of vernal pools, but cured in campfire smoke.

"I can't believe we've never met," said Journeyman, feeling stupid. Eke and Astur moved the last of the provisions into her boat. Astur hurried. Journeyman could tell she liked this wind.

"I'm not surprised," said Walt, grinning. "I never got off the back of my horse, few times I come down here."

Eke and Walt huddled inside the cockpit's coaming, sheltering from the water. These were not boating men. Journeyman wondered at the helplessness that might overtake them, stranded on an island. Once off the Tinderwick mooring, halfway across to the island, the two leaned together, blunt hands joining, Eke's head on Walt's shoulder. Journeyman tried to look away, but the cold autumn sun dazzled on the water, forcing his gaze back into the boat. Astur, turning from her steady labor at the tiller, smiled.

Eke and Walt nuzzled, whispered into each other's beards. Was it Todbaum and his coffee that had uncorked them? Journeyman knew that made no sense. He felt himself pining for a chance with Drenka. He could wish this one thing in the world unarrested, if nothing else.

Astur moored near the island. The four of them transferred the sailboat's contents and themselves to a scow, then oared their way through the field of rockweed surrounding the island until their feet found purchase on the slimy rock.

Eke and Walt dragged their tent and provisions up along the beach. The rest they left for others to convey up from the cove. For others were here, Journeyman saw now.

49.

HALF THE TOWN, AND HIS SISTER TOO

JOURNEYMAN MOVED UP FROM THE beach. Renee and Ernesto and other Spodosolians greeted him with casual cheer. Mike Raritan too. Raritan never missed a *many-hands-make-light-work* chance, a Grange repainting or greenhouse raising. All had come on an earlier boat, to help shift lumber up into the island's growth, toward its rocky summit. It lay scattered just above the high-tide mark on the rocks, repurposed hand-chiseled beams and joists from the peninsula's collapsed barns, those nineteenth-century specimens sagging to rest on their stone foundations. The old lumber had been loaded onto a scow for use in Astur's lighthouse project, on the island's highest bluff.

The rock teemed with activity. Journeyman shouldn't have been surprised at finding Maddy here as well. She'd let Astur be the public face of the project, kept herself oblique. But Journeyman shouldn't be fooled.

Maddy seemed exalted out in the daylight. "Sandy!" When his sister called his name like that, Journeyman was thrown back to Rehoboth Beach. Ankles-deep in the sucking surf, watching his sister tilt into the waves, feeling terror for her that she didn't feel herself.

Parents high on the dunes in aluminum chaise lounges, their father with a book across his face. Journeyman might have been ten or eleven when he realized his younger sister was a better and braver swimmer than he was, and always would be.

"Lift with your knees." Maddy positioned herself at one end of a barn beam, indicating Journeyman should take the other. The Spodosolians were shifting the titanic beams onto wheelbarrows, to thread up along the narrow path into the trees. Journeyman took her commands, including lifting from his knees.

"Who's tending your garden?" he shouted to her from the other end of the beam.

"Maybe one of my interns," she said. She'd used this word to taunt Journeyman since the day he'd once made the mistake of using it in her presence. He'd been referring to the aspiring writers pressed into service around a writer's room in which he'd been a senior member. A standard term. When none of her farming collective was in hearing, she used it to needle him.

"Your interns all seem to be here today," Journeyman said. So far as he could tell, this was true.

"Why don't you let me worry about that. Who's killing your ducks?"

"Augustus is done for the week," he said. "Anyway, I don't kill ducks, I just clean up the blood."

"I can't believe you said that."

"What?"

"It's just so perfectly you, Sandy. That distinction. 'I just clean up the blood.'"

"You can come help me one of these days and it won't seem so allegorical or whatever it is you're suggesting with that tone. It's food, for people to eat."

"If I ate them, I'd kill them myself."

"You eat the eggs," he said, lamely.

They made their way uphill with the barn beam, Maddy guiding the wheelbarrow backward, Journeyman shepherding the over-hanging weight from behind. The island's paths were no wider than the span of the wheelbarrow's handles; they grazed branches at every bend. Yet the century-old paths, though laced with roots, were tamped smooth, never more than they could bump over. Ahead, Eke and Walt sprang like goats into the pathless trees. They'd arrived at their new home. Astur and Maddy's design, Journeyman thought. Their script.

At the top the scene opened. That which Journeyman hadn't had the vision to conceive. Half of East Tinderwick had been enlisted. Specifically the half not magnetized to the goings-on in Founder's Park, to Todbaum's stories. Here was Paulo, Dodie Metzger. Delia Limetree, with Danny, the remaining twin. Mike Raritan, who'd preceded them up the hill. They arrayed like hive insects on the sun-scrubbed granite bluff, studying the foundation that had begun to be assembled out of those sheared blocks abandoned as imperfect by the quarrymen so long ago.

Here was Ed Waltz, so rarely far from his barn full of contraptions. Today he'd exported his steam-powered welding torch to the island, and labored at the assembly of a giant hinged clamshell vise. Like the mouth of a Venus flytrap, one large enough to gulp down an elephant. Here, too, was Nils, never ordinarily far from his bicycles. He worked on a thing like an enormous derailleur, a pulley-and-chain system, a black-greased ruin Journeyman recognized as salvaged from the container bridge at the old dock. Even Jane and Lucius had come. Rare to see them in bright daylight. Both had their sleeves rolled and, with Astur, worked slapping nails into tar shingles on the roof of a new-assembled shack. A storage shed? Living quarters for Eke and Walt?

Journeyman felt included-out. This was a conspiracy he'd missed. It stung at an old wound he'd forgotten he bore. Would he forever be defined as "from away," an accidental member of the community? His lasting presence here merely a symptom of the Arrest?

"I went on a date," he heard himself brag to his sister.

"Really? That's terrific, Sandy. You meet online?"

"Funny."

"I don't know, I thought maybe your old friend has Tinder in his wondermobile."

"Supercar," he corrected.

"Tinder in his supercar, then."

"If he does, he's hoarding it."

"Okay, so spill the beans. A date with who? Person, place, or vegetable?"

"You don't know her. The woman who moved into the library. She's odd, a little intense. But, you know, I make my rounds. She's warmed up to me. Even the odd and intense need human contact, I guess."

"Drenka, you mean?"

"You know her?"

"We've met," said Maddy simply.

Journeyman hid his disappointment. He'd wanted this one thing to himself.

It wasn't difficult to hide. Maddy had turned from him again. Not merely flinched from his gaze, though she had done that. This was the deep interior barricade, a thing for which Journeyman felt an ancestral recognition. A thing to which he'd learned to defer. On the beaches at Rehoboth, so long ago, his sister only sometimes beckoned to him to join her in deeper waters. Other times she'd dive beneath, not beckoning at all, and swim where Journeyman couldn't imagine following.

50.

WHAT WERE THEY BUILDING UP THERE?

JOURNEYMAN DIDN'T KNOW, BUT IT worked on him in his dreams. These recurred night after night. In them he approached the island by boat, but not Astur's sailboat. He was on the prow of some larger thing. A ferry? In the dreams the boat was to his back, a wedge riding high and steady in the surf, but he sensed it beneath him, rather than seeing it. It approached the island with no apparent method of slowing, or plan to divert from the inevitable collision, but Journeyman never experienced fear, only fascination. His attention remained locked on the thing under construction high on the bluff.

The tower or pylon or ziggurat.

Other times it seemed some kind of titanic effigy or golem.

Perhaps a rocket on its pad, an Apollo finger pointing through clouds, to the exosphere.

Yet the monument underway was a lighthouse—yes? Why not believe Astur's declarations? Well, for one thing, what Journeyman had witnessed in progress that day, the day of Eke and Walt's release to their captivity, didn't resemble any lighthouse he knew. For another thing, what powered a lighthouse now? What beacon or battery could generate the signal, in the long night of the Arrest?

And, though Journeyman sailed to the island occasionally, he spent more time by far with the thing in his dreams.

It was night as he approached, and yet, according to the laws of dream, the tower project was always blindingly backlit by the sun. High noon at midnight, on this inner-island. He'd struggle to make out the form within the nimbus of light. Like a phosphene, a blot on his vision, he seemed never to be quite facing it directly. When he turned, it turned too, following him like a moon.

Was that a face he saw?

Was it on fire, this tower? Wreathed in smoke? Were birds above it, wheeling?

Did it fall toward Journeyman, or he toward it?

III.

WINTER

51.

CUSTODY

JEROME KORMENTZ HAD PREPARED THE tableau, Journeyman could see, well in advance of his arrival. He'd built a large fire in his stone pit by the shore of the Lake of Tiredness. Journeyman had to admire Kormentz's beaverishness, not only in gathering the wood and tinder necessary to warm himself out-of-doors but in constructing at the water's edge a lean-to, an entirely new structure, albeit modest. Perhaps Kormentz had caught the bug of industry running wild on Quarry Island. It had grown more intense with the onset of winter.

Kormentz welcomed Journeyman into his sitting hut, and poured some floral concoction from a teapot into mugs without handles. A stack of manuscript pages lay pinned beneath a rounded heavy stone. The topmost page displayed Kormentz's precise cursive hand.

"Your book," Journeyman said. *The Pillow Book*, of course.

"Yes."

Journeyman sat, sheltering from the chill that had found him as he'd emerged from the tree-tight path. Doing so placed him with

Kormentz in a kind of love seat. Later, this too seemed a feature of his scrupulous attentions in making this scene. The lean-to captured the heat coming out of the ring of stones admirably well. The pages lay between them, rippling in the breeze.

"Is it finished?"

"Such a book is never finished, only abandoned."

Journeyman shut his eyes, deeply irritated, though he knew he'd walked into that one.

"Well, it looks . . . sizable."

"I'm placing it in your custody," Kormentz said.

"Oh?"

"To take with you, to your island. That makes you my literary executor, should I perish." Journeyman stared. "Are you surprised?"

"I came today expecting we'd talk about the island," he said, with caution. "You're a little ahead of me."

"Sandy, please. In this time of illusion, shouldn't we dispense with any prevarication between us, my dear confessor?"

"Okay." *Dispense* likely meant, with Kormentz, its opposite. Journeyman hadn't seen Kormentz so high on his own theatrical solemnities since the time of his expulsion from East Tinderwick.

"You don't imagine you're the only one who comes here to talk, do you?"

"I knew it was possible we weren't exclusive," Journeyman deadpanned. "Do you want to tell me who it is?"

"I'm bound not to."

One of Kormentz's allies, from the period of deliberation over his fate? A traumatized former acolyte? Even after their guru's exile, Journeyman knew how bound some had remained. Perhaps Kormentz even had a lover. Journeyman refused to be interested.

"Is this person inside your house right now? Is that why we're out here in the cold?"

"No, they're not inside my house. Please, don't patronize me. I know the news."

"Rumors, you mean."

"Call it what you like. I'm aware of the planned retreat. And that I've been sacrificed."

"For god's sake, Jerome, you haven't been sacrificed."

52.

NEWS AND RUMORS

THAT THE CORDON FROM THE south had scheduled an assault. That it would occur in these light-dwindled days before the solstice.

That the first objective of the assault was the seizure of Todbaum's vehicle.

That the objective had expanded. That the Cordon had determined to seize one or several of the essential farms supplying them with rations.

That Spodosol Ridge Farm was the Cordon's principal target. This, because the Cordon's nemesis Todbaum had named it as his destination. That Spodosol was seen as complicit with Todbaum. That now the farmers had a weapon, and might use it against the Cordon.

That the Cordon planned what was called a "surgical strike."

That there were factions among the Cordon people. That some preferred a more "scorched-earth" approach.

That secret negotiations were being conducted on a "back channel." That the Cordon had planted "moles" amid the towns.

That Quarry Island was being prepared as a defensible redoubt, for a last stand. That the new structures were meant as refugee shelters for Spodosolians and East Tinderwickians during the coming assault (the "retreat" to which Kormentz had referred). That, despite obvious materials limits (on roofs, beds, provisions), safe harbor had been offered to anyone in East Tinderwick, or even Tinderwick proper, who cared to ask.

That, conversely, harbor had been offered only to those on a select list, in a process undemocratic and nontransparent. That Jerome Kormentz had been singled out for exclusion.

That the retreat to the island had been conceived on the principles of nonviolent resistance.

That such principles were laughably misapplied here, in an overreaction by newcomers unaccustomed to local ways of resolving conflict. That the struggle over Todbaum and his supercar should be recast as a dispute between neighbors to be settled in the "old manner" (which remained unspecified).

That the retreat to the island amounted to nothing so much as a mass suicide (both "lemmings" and "Masada" were invoked here).

That the retreat to the island was a daring last-chance military stratagem.

That what was under construction on the island was not a lighthouse but in fact a gigantic slingshot or trebuchet. That the fantastical crab claws Ed Waltz had been welding were intended for the gripping of giant chunks of granite, to be hurled over the water at attackers daring to set sail from the shore.

That Peter Todbaum was about to make the entire thing moot by pulling up his watering tube and nuclear-powering his way out of their lives.

That he'd start for Canada or set out across the ocean. That he was about to instruct the supercar to burrow into the earth, to tunnel and conceal itself, to lurk like unexploded ordnance.

That Todbaum was in league with the Cordon. That together they'd scripted the entire episode as a kind of pantomime to outflank the towns.

That Todbaum was terrified and had gratefully accepted the promise of the towns' defense of him on the island.

That Todbaum had gone crazy.

That Todbaum was crazy to start with.

These things could not all simultaneously be the case. Journeyman could if he chose confirm a few pieces. That some number of people were prepared to fall back to the island, yes. That Kormentz had been, like the unicorn stranded by Noah's ark, denied passage—though Journeyman didn't admit this to Kormentz, it was true.

Some ignored or denied such talk. Others, on the margins, deepwoodsers, might have been blissfully ignorant. If you hadn't seen the boats going out, or the tower rising, it might have been hard to believe. Threat of the Cordon's seizure of the farms wasn't new. It floated in the air, an ambient thing.

As for Todbaum, that wrongness had rooted in their midst. A glitch or tumor, a television tuned to a dead channel in a world where there were no televisions tuned to any channels. The peninsula's reality had grown around Todbaum, absorbed him.

53.

THE WORTH OF RITUAL ACTION

NOW KORMENTZ GOGGLED HIS EYES. The whites wholly visible around the pupils, the rims red, the bonfire reflected in their centers. Journeyman saw rage and terror, all that Kormentz labored never to reveal.

"Take the book, Sandy. It's what remains of me. It mustn't fall into their hands." He gripped the pages with his bony claws, causing Journeyman to think of the giant steel pincers under construction out at Quarry Island. As he thrust the manuscript at Journeyman's chest, he dislodged the stone which had pinned the pages. It fell to the ground between them. Journeyman accepted the unbound book into his care, reluctantly.

"Take it," Kormentz said again. "Or I'll put it into the fire myself."

"They'll march right past the turnoff to the lake," Journeyman said. "They have no interest in you."

Kormentz managed a bitter smile. "How certain you are."

"What could they want from you? Or your book?"

"They'll want this place for a northern outpost."

"They'll take the Grange." Was it possible they'd already done so? With Quentin Maslow gone, no one lived at the North Grange to report otherwise. At the last drop-off the Cordon people had stayed after, while Journeyman returned to Tinderwick.

"An outpost *out of sight of the road*," Kormentz said.

Outpost? Journeyman suddenly wondered at the martial terminology. Could Kormentz's secret visitor be from the Cordon?

In these paranoid days, Journeyman tried not to take the bait. "Fair enough. Maybe they'll put you in charge of it. As the northern sentry you can write to your heart's content."

"Take it now and go," Kormentz said. "I only hope my faith in you isn't misplaced. They're coming here to pillage and destroy."

"Destroy what?" said Journeyman. "They need the farms."

"What they don't need they'll sacrifice. They'll surely kill me and cast my book into the lake or the fire."

"Seems a little extreme." Journeyman reconsidered his worry, that Kormentz had formed some tricky alliance. The disgraced guru could never join up with the Cordon. All of Kormentz's pretenses and allusions, his arch piety, needed the context of the community that had banished him to lend them any meaning at all.

"Yes," Kormentz said, his gaze fierce. "It is extreme. Deny it at your peril."

"Deny what?"

"The destructive impulse. How little you grasp the worth of ritual action. It's your principal failing, Sandy."

Kormentz waved his hand. Shed of his book, he seemed also to want to discharge Journeyman. As Kormentz stood, to toss wood onto his bonfire, Journeyman noticed what he hadn't before: the fuel supply included the legs and backs of two or three shattered chairs, and the remains of an antique bookstand. Kormentz hadn't only been clearing brush. He'd begun burning the furniture.

Journeyman walked into the stiff wind, up from the lake, Kormentz's manuscript in his bag. Was it Journeyman's job to read it? Show it to others? He could destroy it, as Kormentz feared the Cordon might. Kormentz had threatened to do so himself; it might be his perverse wish. He'd given no instructions, anyhow, other than that Journeyman should take it to the island. It wasn't as though there was publication anymore, or posterity. Or maybe there was only posterity? Perhaps Kormentz had outsmarted it. Perhaps he'd named names, thinking that after the Arrest, and the world's collapse into locality, no one would ever wish to read a book in which they didn't themselves appear.

54.

PUNTERS

SOMETHING HAD CHANGED IN DECEMBER. The worst thing a Hollywood producer could imagine: the shrinkage of his audience. Todbaum still had Theodore Nowlin, true. Nowlin was unshakable. Teenagers still used the park, yes, but was it Journeyman's imagination, or didn't they seem as interested in Todbaum now? Maybe Todbaum had only ever been an occasion to them. An excuse.

The rest of his listeners had gone, shortly after the story of the woman named Pittsburgh. That tale seemed in retrospect to have marked a change in the tone of Todbaum's narrations—a watershed, a climax or anticlimax. At first his regulars puttered through the park, possibly feeling guilty at making too abrupt a break from the storytelling evenings. They'd take a cup of coffee or leave an offering, some firewood or food, then excuse themselves. Soon enough, they forgot to come at all. This coincided with the quickening pulse of construction of the whatever-it-was. Visiting Founder's Park, Journeyman saw boat traffic, bodies and lumber and machinery crossing to Quarry Island, no matter the wind or weather.

It had turned to winter now, even in this winter-challenged world.

The change at the park was self-fulfilling. The fewer the listeners, the less motive for Todbaum to weave long threads. That was if he was still capable. Journeyman wasn't sure. Todbaum's descriptions of what was "out there" now folded on themselves, became paradoxical and gnomic. It was less a serial, more a run of half-baked existentialist fugues. Todbaum had made that error of which Journeyman never thought him capable: building to a proper cliffhanger, he'd digress, burning momentum and good faith. After journeying coast to coast, his skirmish with the Cordon ought to have been his payoff, his money shot. Any storyteller knew this. Only Todbaum didn't seem to want to *tell* it.

"You know what's funny?" Todbaum said. Journeyman had pressed him on the point. They sat alone at the fire, isolated in a morning fog, hands warming around Todbaum's coffee. The sea's vapor was so thick Journeyman couldn't make out the island. "I don't even know what it was I did to tick off your homeboys. I was *asleep.*"

"What do you mean?"

"I was drunk, Sandy. I'd plundered a hoard of liquor outside Worcester. These dudes were hiding it in a shed. Cheap shit, a few liters of Popov and a case of hard cider in bottles, real sweet. Tasted better mixed, and by 'better' I mean than camel piss. I was feeling experimental, and when I hit on this unholy mixed beverage I decided to experiment with drinking myself to death. Just about emptied the supply over a day and a night. Time got a little slippery after that."

"Outside Worcester?"

"That's the thing, Sandy. I was on autopilot by then, locked in on your little sanctuary. I felt heedless, sick of ducking and weaving. Route 495, skirting Boston—I never did get a look at what had become of Boston—and then 95. Straight up the chute, what's the big deal? I figured the Streak could handle it. It was up around Portsmouth when I blacked out."

"And?"

"Came to under the kindly ministrations of a maddened-up bunch of your shit-cyclists."

Journeyman glanced at the supercar then, involuntarily. Todbaum had been exiting it more often, though he never ranged far. He seemed to like the gazebo's fringe of high grass for his urinations, saving his shitting for the Streak's built-in eco-toilet, which Todbaum had boasted of but Journeyman had never seen. These days Todbaum liked to climb down and take his coffee by the fire, as though trying to repopulate his open-air theater with his own presence. Journeyman recalled how, long ago, Todbaum used to prefer the British term "punters" for the paying customer. He liked the separation it gave him and whichever listener he flattered—to speak of punters was never to be one.

Maybe, Journeyman thought now, Todbaum wanted distance from the Blue Streak. Had the supercar's luminosity increased? Its aura was noticeable now even in this fog-diffused daylight. Yet if Todbaum feared the Streak's radiation, his lead-lined cockpit was the one place to be. Maybe he feared something less measurable: the supercar's sway over him. His dependence. Maybe he emerged to test the possibility of separation. His readiness to surrender his exoskeleton, become a bare forked root again. Yet if he threw himself on the towns' mercy, he'd be a punter forever. Todbaum had never yet been inside a single one of their homes. Had he been sheltered in a building once, since setting out from Malibu? Had he been invited to be?

The next evening they sat alone again by the fire, Journeyman and Todbaum. Two teenagers made out on the floor of the gazebo, possibly fucked, under a blanket. Journeyman wondered, not for the first time, what this world was to them. How did they remember a time before the Arrest? Journeyman sat with his back to this scene, while Todbaum unabashedly stared.

"Have you thought of simply handing the car over?" Journeyman ventured. "Just walk away?"

"Over to whom?"

"The Cordon."

"I'd like to see those fucking yahoos try to occupy the Streak. Thing hates them like the plague. Why do you think it went berserk while I was in my stupor, Sandman? They should consider themselves lucky. I was the only thing holding it off."

"The supercar can hate?"

"It's an AI, which means it's capable of learning, unlike those bozos."

This struck Journeyman as thin. Schoolyard stuff, practically— *you and what army, my car is smarter than your entire Cordon*, etc. Journeyman's skepticism rose, hearing Todbaum toss off a term like "AI." Having collaborated on a futuristic narrative for more than a decade, Journeyman knew the limits on Todbaum's interest in, or grasp of, technology. It had always been Journeyman's hands on the keyboard. Todbaum was incapable of so much as installing an update to Final Draft without summoning a flunky.

"Does it talk to you?" Journeyman asked. "I mean, if it's learning, does it know you're there?"

"Sure, we talk."

"I'd like to hear that sometime." Perhaps it was finally Journeyman's turn to needle Todbaum. "Or do you do both voices, really, like a ventriloquist?"

Todbaum obliged with his ready defensiveness. "Fuck off, Sandy."

"So you're protecting us from it? Who are its favorites? How does it feel about *me?*"

"Worse by the minute. For instance, it knows you never handed off my contract to your sister."

Journeyman ignored this. They both knew it was true. "Is the Streak rivalrous?" he asked Todbaum. "Have you got it working on a screenplay? Does it take notes well? Has it solved the third act problems?"

Todbaum laughed insanely. He never stayed defensive for long. Still, Journeyman pressed on.

"You don't know the first thing, do you? It's a black box, like an iPhone. You're just a *client* of the thing. Maybe it's the ventriloquist and you're the dummy."

Todbaum's laugh shrank to a low, mean murmur. "I know more about it than anyone ever will. It'll kill you if you try to take the wheel. God help me, Sandy, don't let me see you try."

"The longer you stare into the Blue Streak, the longer the Blue Streak stares into you, huh? The Blue Streak, *c'est moi?*"

"Something like that."

"So, what does it see?"

"Eh?" Todbaum's gaze was locked on the teenagers beneath their blanket, if only to keep from meeting Journeyman's.

"If you know the car and the car knows you, *who's in there?* You ran over a lot of bodies out in flyover country, stole some food and booze, handed out coffee. In your journeys, have you met yourself yet?"

"Aw, Sandman, you disappoint me."

"How's that?"

"'Self' is a shuck, my friend. Have I taught you nothing?"

"A shuck?"

"Ersatz. Fool's gold. The self's a howling counterfeit, an arena where no show goes on, a parenthesis with nothing inside. You used to know it, Sandy. In college, I remember you once said, 'Everyone's secrets are the same.' Look at those kids." He meant up at the gazebo. Journeyman refused to turn.

"I'm not sure that what I meant was 'The self's a shuck.'"

"Sure it is. It's a vacancy. You can decorate it with distinctive stuff. Neurosis. Like a fingerprint or a snowflake, no two alike. But that's like tattoos on an arm. What do they call it, a 'sleeve tattoo'? You can embroider the whole damn container. Beneath the decoration, a nullity. Like outer space, mostly dark stuff."

"Dark matter," Journeyman corrected, mechanically. Cleaning up Todbaum's syntactic messes and stray signifiers was Journeyman's old avocation.

"Yeah, dark matter. That's the majority, right? Ninety percent of everything, including you and me, and the Blue Streak too. Who knows why any of us do anything? You remember the story about the scorpion and the frog crossing the river?"

"Please don't tell it again." The scorpion stung the frog, Journeyman recalled, because it was *in his nature*. "Doesn't that story indicate the opposite, anyway? That the self is some kind of ineradicable essence?"

"Keep it simple, stupid. The lesson is we're all dumb destructive monkeys in the dark."

Kormentz's word: *destructive*. The destructive impulse. Maybe Todbaum and the man at the Lake of Tiredness really were two peas in a pod.

Now, using his sporadic talent for reading Journeyman's mind, Todbaum said, "Buddhism, that's the dumbest shit in the world, I always thought."

"I don't follow."

"Getting away from the self, as if there's anything to get away from. Same with that Keatsian *whatchamacallit*; you used to go on about it in college. Negative capability! Like it's some kind of accomplishment, not knowing, always guessing, pretzeling yourself in contradiction. There isn't anything *but* negative capability, Sandy. It's pouring out of your dumb face right now, like Niagara Falls."

Journeyman was bludgeoned to silence by Todbaum's Rube Goldberg allusions. All were melted into worthless slag by the time he'd finished with them. Out here, by a dying fire, under winter-bright stars, on the periphery of the human story: leave it to Todbaum to hold a grudge against *negative capability* at this late date.

55.

NOWLIN'S PLAN

JUST THEN JOURNEYMAN WAS JOLTED by the apparitional figure of Theodore Nowlin, who suddenly tossed a length of pine onto the fire, causing a brief vortex of sparks. Had Nowlin been listening? He was silent for such long stretches that Journeyman could forget he was there. He'd become Todbaum's patriarchal spirit guide.

"Can't let 'em have it," Nowlin said now, a stoical grunt.

"Sorry?" Journeyman said.

"Can't let 'em have it," Nowlin repeated. "Need it for the passage out. We're going to Brunswick, me and your friend. You ought to come along."

Journeyman looked to Todbaum, who gave the thumbs-up. "It's a plan, Stan."

"Couldn't get anyone to build a boat, for all the pride in boat-building," said Nowlin. "But Mr. Todbaum's caught the spirit. He says it's good to go."

"The Streak swims?" Journeyman asked.

Todbaum shook his head. "Uh-uh. Crawls along the bottom. Remember, it's built on the bones of a tunnel-boring machine."

"You've *done* this?"

"I forded the Mississippi."

A story Journeyman missed, if Todbaum had told it. "Bath Harbor's a lot farther away than the width of the Mississippi River. Deeper too."

"We're planning a test run," said Todbaum. And—did Journeyman imagine it?—Todbaum winked, across the fire. "I thought we'd go out to Quarry Island, and crawl back out for an inspection. If all's watertight, we'll press on to find Theodore's community in Brunswick."

Could Todbaum seriously care to undertake such a voyage, on Nowlin's behalf? Or was the scheme a baroque cover for his wish to decamp to Quarry Island after all? He'd only have to get that far, then declare that the Blue Streak had sprung a leak. There he'd be, parked in the midst of Maddy and Astur's new settlement, sticking his feeding tube deep into the island's bedrock.

Journeyman tried to gather his wits. This was information, one way or another. He'd been so beguiled into abstraction—*neurosis an embroidery covering a void! Negative capability!*—that he'd missed the swerve into logistical fact. The plan must have been the source for the rumor that the Blue Streak was capable of tunneling underground. Theodore Nowlin would have spread this idea by bragging in town about the coming expedition.

Why so grudging, when it came to Nowlin's plan? Yes, Journeyman found the man tedious. Tedious, and crazily wrong about what might be found, should he ever manage to persuade anyone to sail with him to Brunswick. Yet Nowlin only proved Maddy's words, by his hunger to connect with distant places gone silent. *Everyone here lost someone.* Journeyman had more in common with Nowlin than he'd care to admit. Like Nowlin, he'd ended up in Todbaum's park when all others were gone.

Nowlin's craziness might be the usual, abject variety: he might simply be lonely. Journeyman was crazy with loneliness, or lonely with craziness; he ought to have sympathy. Some days, Journeyman thought the *world* had been crazy and tried to go sane: that was the Arrest.

Todbaum, on the other hand, wasn't crazy, not like the rest of them, not like a person. Todbaum, with his confusions of self and surround, of author and text, was craziness itself. Perhaps that was why his car—which was also a phone and a gun and a mirror, one of those spooky devices everyone dreamed over—still worked. The question was this: Was Todbaum's arrival, the Blue Streak's existence, evidence that the Arrest hadn't taken root? That it was all coming back?

56.

JOURNEYMAN'S AFFILIATIONS

THESE DAYS, THOSE BESIDES NOWLIN actively shunned the park. Likely they feared being roped into a last stand on behalf of Todbaum. The stories had tailed off, into paradox and self-loathing. Erratic, uninspiring, Todbaum made no apparent preparations, not for battle, nor for keeping his weird promise to embark with Nowlin. The supercar sat ominously inert, ever glowing, exchanging waste for moisture and nutrient from the park's lawn, which had begun to yellow and stink. Was it Journeyman's imagination or was the Streak's perimeter slightly concaved, as though a sinkhole had begun to form?

Quarry Island was the active concern. The tower visible from shore now, nosing above the trees. Smoke and steam drifted up too. An onshore wind might bring a scent of cooking, something delicious being savored by the workers. Were there permanent residents apart from Eke and Walt? Journeyman didn't believe so. But Nils, so utterly caught up with Ed Waltz in construction of the crab-armed mechanism, had pitched a tent on the island's far shore, and spent nights there. Bicycles could rot for the time being.

Journeyman rarely crossed. He still had rounds. Augustus was sympathetic to the ongoing efforts, yet still needed butchering help. Journeyman spread himself thin, racing on his bicycle to hit marks in many places at once. He had no role on the island. Instead he worked the shoreside, schlepped wheelbarrows full of stuff to the put-in, sent over packets of Victoria's sausages. Hoping that, or his family relation, should be enough to count him among the saved, when the axe fell.

All felt this, though no one spoke of it—the axe was soon to fall.

But the problem of Journeyman's affiliations wasn't simply binary, island or park. He fretted: Why did Drenka so rarely leave the library? What would it mean to be in hiding, after the Arrest? And from whom?

"You'd be welcome at Quarry Island," Journeyman told her, on his own authority. "It's good company. And it's beautiful out there." They sat on the library's back step in bright cold sunlight, sharing shrimp with black bean sauce, spicy and astringent, from a scratched and beaten Tupperware container. Lucius was as skilled at Szechuan cuisine as French. He'd cooked it at the island's new brick woodstove. A marvel, the miniature civilization now assembled there. Lucius ferried the leftovers back that morning, on Astur's boat, surprising Journeyman with them. This might be a watershed moment: the island feeding the mainland.

"No thanks," Drenka said.

Journeyman waited. She didn't elaborate. "You can go later, if you want." *Or have to.* He enjoyed a dumb throb of valor, imagining securing her a spot on the last boat leaving.

Journeyman thought to tell Drenka that she'd like his sister but remembered the two had already met, and fell silent.

Drenka solved the problem of speech by taking him and kissing him, then, a bright shock of tongue and ginger-scallion breath. The kiss wasn't repeated. They parted without mentioning it. Yet, still,

Journeyman felt the whisper of a more private affiliation. Though Drenka had promised him nothing, he felt for the first time since the Arrest the chance that he, Journeyman—dialogue polisher, duck-blood rinser, emissary, older-brother-fifth-wheel-sidekick—might locate the constituency of himself.

57.

NO TRUMPETS

IT BEGAN WITH A PICNIC. The ruins of a picnic, a fire circle in the first snow. Perhaps they'd crossed in, a day or two earlier, and camped, Eke-and-Walt-style, in the woods. Who could say? The towns kept no perimeter watch. The line was somewhere high beyond the North Grange, and the line belonged to the Cordon. The towns had no spies or sentries who'd report when it was crossed.

The butcher, Augustus Cordell, told Journeyman. He'd learned from someone at Proscenium Farm. The remains of a fire in the snow had been found in one of Proscenium's back fields, behind the creek's tree line, past the farm's wallows. The scorched skull and carcass of one of their hogs, scattered bones, a smashed jug or two. Scanning for traces, they'd also found the scene of the hog's slaughter. Gore and entrails at the creek's edge. The butcher shook his head. It appeared to have been done with a timber axe, one found missing from the Proscenium barns. Calling up this image seemed to trouble Augustus most, the clumsy murder of the hog. It wasn't right.

There was no need for them to come in waves, nor come noisily, with trumpets. No need to inspire shock and awe. They'd filtered in. Housed who-knew-where, at encampments, stealthily seized houses. Perhaps they had sympathizers? Those who gladly offered lodging? Who'd have any way of knowing? Yet at some point they did set up a block on the road. Journeyman was met with it, two days later, trying to bring provisions to Jerome Kormentz.

Snow lay in patches between the shading pines. It melted on the roadbed. The frost was incomplete, no new heaves. The asphalt's fissures were the old ones, the geological record. The crows that tailed Journeyman might have been the old ones too: What would be the point of new crows? What if, despite the seasons' turning, they'd all been Arrested, too, heaves and crows and persons, never aging, trapped in some purgatorial recursion? Journeyman would bring Kormentz packages forever, perhaps. Like his *Pillow Book*, a world that could never be finished, only abandoned.

But no. Here was the new thing on the road. A shed plopped onto the center of it, at the bend before Brenda's Folly Farm. A prefab aluminum toolshed, barely larger than a porta potty. In the days of pickup trucks such things were purchased at Lowe's and plopped onto one's lawn in an hour or two. Journeyman imagined them sledging it all the way up from their territories south of here. He marveled at the effort. But no, a foolish thought. Likely the shed was from nearby, repurposed off some Tinderwickian's property, dragged behind the Cordon's horses a mile at most. A drift of smoke tooted from its rooftop vent. No sign of horses or bikes or shit-bikes anywhere near, though Journeyman had hardly inspected the surroundings.

Two men, one he knew by sight from the meeting at the North Grange and, before, from encounters on the road. Not that it mattered. Names went unexchanged, let alone pleasantries. The two warmed their hands at a fire in a small ceramic barrel. Despite the vent, smoke would have made the air unbreathable if the door hadn't been propped open—it was bad even so.

"Stand right there," said the one Journeyman had never seen before.

"Sure." There wasn't room for Journeyman inside anyhow. There were no weapons, such as he could judge, inside the shed.

The man looked him up and down. "You ought to hand that off and make your way back south." This man chewed something that made a brownish juiciness glisten between his teeth, a wad of bound leaves—could it really be tobacco? Journeyman wondered if he was some official of significance within their ranks.

"There's a man at the lake—" he started.

"We know."

"This food's for him. He'll be expecting it."

"He's good," said the same one. The one Journeyman had seen before looked down at his boots. "We got your man taken care of."

"He's expecting *me*," he said. "He'll be surprised—"

"Then let him be surprised." The man reached out.

Journeyman began reluctantly to remove Kormentz's provisions from the pack.

"Whole thing'll do."

"Sorry?"

"Your satchel, just leave it."

Journeyman's Telluride Film Festival backpack. It had journeyed with him across the divide of the Arrest. Part of the cornucopia of swag waiting in his hotel room in that mountain town. He'd fanned the treasure on his bedspread just to marvel: hand lotions, sleep masks, thumb drives, cranberry-pistachio clusters, chargers for charging other chargers, all branded by Dolby or Rotten Tomatoes or Variety or some other festival sponsor. All those monikers and devices now gone, gone, gone. Journeyman handed it over. *Choose your battles*, he thought. Had he ever chosen even one?

"That's a good man," the Cordon man said, as to a dog. Then added, obscurely, "Much obliged to your service."

Journeyman set out back down the road, relieved of his burden. A delivery boy, he'd delivered. Or had he been mugged in broad daylight on the frost-heaved boulevard?

The crow shadowing him tree to tree might know.

58.

THE LAST AMERICAN

UNMOORED, EMBARRASSED TO RETURN TO the butcher's, Journeyman staggered through the empty streets downtown, past the library. No sign of life there. He didn't linger, didn't test for an unlatched door. He walked to the docks behind the firehouse. Heaps of lobster traps waited there for no appointment. The local lobstermen had once peddled their catch for airlift by the thousands to Paris, for the Christmas table. The urchin fishermen, similarly, packed the chewy tasteless things off to Japan, where urchin was known as a cure for erectile dysfunction. Journeyman's mind wandered to such lost worlds as if he could reverse engineer the Arrest. As if it made sense to want to. A spit of woodland concealed the beach where Drenka had abandoned her rowboat. Perhaps it was no longer there, perhaps she'd rowed off. Multiple disasters tickled the edges of Journeyman's awareness. When the sun set and he grew cold, he remembered Todbaum. He was Journeyman's to feed. Todbaum had an appetite.

Journeyman fetched his bicycle. After his encounter on the main road he wanted to be able to outpace anyone on foot. He'd find dinner at Spodosol for himself, and a share to deliver to Todbaum. The peninsula felt vacant, haunted at sunset. If not a hot meal, then something from Spodosol's stores. Whatever he fetched could be heated at Todbaum's fire. If he had a fire.

Journeyman stopped at the top of Founder's Park before reaching the Spodosol road. Todbaum had a fire. He also had something to eat. He sat on a lawn chair scooping food from a bowl held near to his chin. Sentinel Nowlin by his side. Likely Nowlin provided the food. A third, Edwin Gorse, stood on the far side of the fire, his anxious gesticulations casting shadows reaching into the bare trees. Almost unconsciously Journeyman dismounted and slow-walked his bicycle in. Should he have felt it his duty to inform Maddy and Astur, others, what he'd encountered on the road—to sound a general alarm, like Paul Revere? Maybe he'd tell Todbaum. Let that satisfy his obligation. It was Todbaum and the Streak they'd presumably come for, those men on the road.

Journeyman's actions weren't sensible, perhaps. He moved benumbed. Things changed, he thought. Then they didn't. And we forgot they could again.

Todbaum and Gorse seemed to be in an argument. "No, no, no, no, no." Todbaum shoveled in chunky soup while grumbling at Gorse across the fire. Beans and potatoes and string beans in tomato broth, a meal that looked Spodosolian to Journeyman. The broth dribbled on Todbaum's unshaven chin. "I don't have to draw the line anywhere, Ed. I never met one single line worth drawing, my man, only crossing."

Lines not worth drawing, only crossing. Hadn't Todbaum said the exact same thing to Journeyman that first night, in a dorm room at Durfee Hall? The feeling was less of déjà vu than of an accordion of years, collapsing. Was Journeyman nothing, through four decades, except Todbaum's dupe, his ratifying witness?

"So, that's your endgame?" Edwin Gorse's tone was sardonic, needling. "That's why you came all this way? To burrow under the ocean floor like a—" His words seemed to fail him.

"Like a pair of ragged claws, exactly."

"And leave us to fight your battles."

"Who's 'us'?" snorted Todbaum. He waved his spoon at the empty park. Theodore Nowlin stood by impassively, watching Todbaum talk and eat. Waiting for his glorious voyage. Did Nowlin eat anymore, or did he give every scrap to Todbaum? Perhaps he lived off the bark of trees.

"Eh?" said Gorse.

"Who's 'us'? Because I don't see anyone much to speak of." Todbaum nodded at Journeyman. "Hey ho, Sandman." Journeyman nodded back. To the others he might have been invisible.

"To have followers, you have to lead," Gorse whined. "Show people what the Streak can do. That's how you got this far."

"What do you know about how I got *anywhere*?" Sucking down the last of the stew, Todbaum tossed the bowl onto the snow-patched grass, then blotted his mouth in the crook of his sleeve.

"You told us, night after night."

"Did I? I could have been shitting you, Ed."

"What do you mean?"

"They're all dead. I just couldn't think of any way to break it to you sensitive types."

"All dead what? How all dead where?" Gorse's syntax seemed to break down, to be broken down, in Todbaum's forge of nonsense. Possibly this had happened to Journeyman, irreversibly, a long while ago.

"It's a wasteland. I mean, not like you imagine, not like I told you. I offered up the consoling fiction, just because I hate to let people down. I love you stupid freaks for keeping on keeping on. It's a human thing, and I like human things. Homely things. What's that German word for it, *heimlich*? Homelike?"

That doesn't mean what you think it means, Journeyman almost said, but didn't.

"So I tried to give you the Heimlich maneuver, har har. I made

up all that total claptrap. There's nothing out there but an irradi-
ated landscape. I never got out of the Streak, for safety's sake, and I
never once drove over anything fresher than a maggot-filled brain-
case with a few scraps of hair, maybe some blackened lips, though
the nose and ears were long eaten off. More often, bleached skulls.
Loads of people died in their cars, and believe me, it is a pain in the
goddamn ass. I twisted through more damn traffic, I steered over
the veritable bones of the moon."

"All dead?"

"Sorry."

"But that doesn't make any sense. The Cordon—"

"Hard to know if they're in on the gag, huh?"

"The gag?"

"People believe what they need to believe. Like you, thinking
your wife's out there somewhere. Am I right, Gorse? That's what
keeps you going, isn't it? The sweet nothing you whisper to those
girls at night when you tuck 'em in?"

"You traveled all the way here to tell us that?"

Todbaum shrugged. "Sure. And for the grub." His gaze flickered
to the emptied bowl in the slushy grass.

"You're saying there is no more America?"

"I'm it, sweetheart. The Last American."

If you meet the Last American on the road, kill him. Another
thought Journeyman didn't utter. The trees that ringed them, they
seemed to beat like quiet hearts.

"You're a liar." Gorse's syntax, if he troubled to notice, was back
on track. "The sky, the fallout—we'd know. And the sea."

"Ha, you got me." Todbaum raised his hands like a Western
villain, but only for an instant. Journeyman suspected he pined for
a better adversary. Gorse was too easy to torture. "That was just the
cover story, but you've proven yourself worthy, Comrade Gorse. You
deserve the truth."

"Go ahead."

"It's all good. Blue skies, shiny happy people. They're laughing their asses off at you dumb hick-topians."

"Who?"

"Everybody, including probably your wife and her new boy toy. They fixed it, everyone's back online, back on the grid. You're living in an experimental preserve, Biosphere Twelve, I think that's what they call it. They pumped the carbon out of the clouds and the sea, everything's hunky-dory now, all nuke-powered VR tech and genetically modified caviar. Sure, the developing world's still fucked, but hey, that's why they call it *developing*. Meanwhile, someone decided to let you guys tough it out just for shits and giggles. Take you at your word, see if you could reinvent the wheel. Like a game of *The Sims*. You *chose* this backwater nirvana, Gorse—don't ask me why. So, you get to live in it. With armed guards at the perimeter. Except you don't even seem to need them. You're obedient, like dogs, stuck behind the invisible fence of your self-regard. This place is a reality show. Only your clicks were down, so they sent me in to goose ratings. Like the way Spider-Man always somehow happens to appear on the cover of every failing comic book."

"*That's* the truth?"

The penultimate truth, Journeyman thought. Another always lay around the corner.

"We lost people. Every one of us lost someone we loved." Maddy's refrain. Journeyman was struck by Gorse's unlikely sense of solidarity, conjured from behind that high hedge.

"They're right where you left 'em," said Todbaum. "Sipping on margaritas and watching Pornhub. And for a punch line, your screwball Erewhon is about to get shrunk down to the size of a single island, and you *still* don't get it. You idiot-ass hippie."

Nowlin stood by, silent as the trees. Why didn't he protest? Was this what he'd been promised, once they burrowed off from Founder's Park? Margaritas and Pornhub?

"So, that's it?" said Gorse. His bitterness was a toxin poisoning only himself. "You crawl off to that island for safety, with the hippies you despise?"

No, Journeyman thought. To renew his proposal to Maddy. Their collaborative venture: to be Adam and Eve of the Unarrest.

"No fucking way. I told you, me and Ted, we're lighting out back to civilization. We'll just drop in on the islanders for a farewell picnic. When the wind's right, I can smell them baking scones from here. Ought to give them one last thrill." Todbaum's mad voice was a fountain to fill the vacuum of night, and the vacuum of himself.

"This entire vehicle's a state-of-the-art recording device, you know. The digital capture of my gallivant through the land of the yahoos ought to keep the punters entertained for weeks, if not months. Time to cash in."

Punters and yahoos, the only two categories of human Todbaum recognized. The yahoos, Journeyman supposed, were those who couldn't even afford to buy a ticket, or a monthly payment to keep their channels lit.

Journeyman had to speak, so at last he did.

"They're here now," he said. "They're out on the road."

"Where?" said Gorse.

"Past Brenda's Folly Farm," he said. "They set up a checkpoint on the road. Though they might be farther south through the woods, on the Drunkard's Path."

"Shit," said Gorse. He stared into the dark, looking panicked. Journeyman supposed he was thinking of his girls. "Can I take your bicycle?"

"Go ahead."

"Run, little man!" shouted Todbaum. "It's time for your close-up!"

Gorse said nothing, just put his back to Todbaum, the Streak, the park. He wobbled on Journeyman's wheels, straightened, was gone.

The Cordon's arrival had stripped Journeyman. Nothing to deliver. Not even a backpack to deliver that nothing with. The night walk to Tinderwick hardly enticed him now. He shared in the fear he'd roused in Gorse: that Tinderwick would be overrun, if it wasn't already. He said his good night and walked the dark path to Spodosol.

59.

YET ANOTHER WORLD, PART 2

IN *YET ANOTHER WORLD,* THE dystopian Earth—the alternate world from which the woman scientist reached out to her boyfriend on the counterpart postapocalyptic Earth—was in sway of a dark global corporation named UnSurAnce. The woman scientist worked at a start-up, helping develop a virtual reality experience called A Room of One's Own, which was proposed as the ultimate in seductive, all-senses-enveloping VR—a product intended, she believed, as a high-end toy. What she didn't know was that her start-up was actually secretly funded—entirely owned, in fact—by UnSurAnce. A Room of One's Own was intended not as a plaything for the wealthy but as a tool for manipulating the dispossessed masses— those unrooted by climate change, the workers made redundant by the onset of robots. The technology was meant to trick them into downloading out of their inconvenient human bodies, to live the remainder of their spans entirely inside a virtual reality mainframe. It was a toy engineered to beguile the user—the *punter*—into paying for the privilege of suicide.

Journeyman crept in. Spodosol was eerily dark. No fires, no lamps, the compound seemingly abandoned. Frightened, tired, he didn't explore. He had no idea where matches and candles were kept. Maddy and Astur were gone. Journeyman curled beneath a woolen blanket on their couch. When he slept, he dreamed of the television show that had never existed. He slept swallowed in his and Todbaum's grim vision. Maddy's too, however little she wished to claim it. Journeyman dreamed he'd entered A Room of One's Own and succumbed, mistaking it for reality. And that now all realms outside its boundary were unavailable to him. Lost.

60.

THE SINKING-UNDER

HE WAS WOKEN IN THE first faint hour of dawn by a body standing over him where he slept, examining him by lamplight.

"I was just sleeping." Journeyman bolted upright in stupid guilt, as though apprehended in the sick indulgence of his dream of virtuality.

"There were signs someone came in at night," Cynthia Pitchings said. "I had to check."

"Where's everyone else?"

"You should get on the boat, Sandy."

"The boat?"

"Astur's rounding up stragglers in an hour or so. You should be down by the water."

"Are you going?"

Cynthia shook her head. "Someone has to stay."

"The captain going down with the farm, eh?"

She grunted. "I'm not going down."

Journeyman found his shoes and coat and followed Cynthia outside. The day was cold, and sparkling. She fed him tea and bread in her own kitchen, then sent him to the boat landing. "Stragglers," it turned out, meant Jane and Lucius. With their love of home comforts, they'd squeezed a last night in their own beds before decamping to the island. Jane carried a tote full of Lucius's kitchen ingredients and some of the heavy French silverware they preferred. Another full of paperback books and a Ziploc bulging with dank buds. With them Journeyman stood and watched Astur first moor, then climb into the rowboat to fetch them from the shore.

"Good morning, friends!" said Astur, when she was near enough to be heard. Despite numberless crossings, her cheer was inexhaustible. Journeyman and Lucius grabbed for the front of her scow, to bring it near and clamber aboard. Jane lifted the canvas bags and conveyed them to Astur for a dry perch on one of the rowboat's seats. Journeyman had nothing, just the clothes he'd slept in. Others, it occurred to him, had been feathering their nests on Quarry Island for weeks now.

"Look," said Jane, when Astur had rowed them nearly to her boat. Jane sat rear-facing. Journeyman and Lucius turned. Across the twinkling water, past the spit of trees separating the launch from Founder's Park, an action was visible at the sand and scrub edge near the gazebo. The supercar, in motion.

"What the fuck," said Lucius.

The Blue Streak had tipped. Waves lightly slapped against its cowcatcher fender. The vehicle dug at the loose grit of the embankment. The juncture where its treads engaged was a blur of dislodged sand. As the wind died, Journeyman made out the whine and whir of its tunneling action, punctuated by hacking and sputtering as its rotors and blades struck fixed stone and entangled with kelp and spiral wrack. Water flooded into the depression where the Blue Streak sank itself deliberately into the beachfront.

"Well would you look at that?" said Jane. "We're in a race to the goddamn island."

Astur clunked the rowboat against her sailboat's stern, then tied on. Only then did she stop to gaze with them at the ferment of sand where the supercar deepened its entrenchment, into the mouth of the bay. She shook her head. "I do not think it will be fast. We should easily win this race."

"Well, that's a relief," said Lucius. His sarcasm died in the open air. It had nothing to stick itself to but their fear. The supercar cratered into the surf and sludge like a monster's cranium. A tumor that had reared from the mire of the world, to which it now returned. They watched it submerge within its own boil, reducing the beachfront to sewage. Journeyman thought of the French boat, the food and shit that had swirled where it sank.

A cry echoed across the water. In the excavation's wake the gushing tide undermined the embankment supporting the put-in ramp. The old beams shrieked a second time, then groaned and split, posts tearing free of the mud, submerged barnacle-white logs bared like a skeleton. Seawater swarmed. The supercar punched this hole in their world, then vanished beneath the froth.

61.

THE FAIRY VILLAGE

WHEN JOURNEYMAN AND HIS SISTER were young, they'd been sent to a summer camp in Maine—William Tell Acres. For two summers Journeyman had gone alone. Then Maddy had joined him, two summers more. The camp formed his only knowledge of Maine, before Maddy drew him back.

When Astur landed them on the island, Journeyman thought of William Tell Acres for the first time since the Arrest. Wending along the close path toward the settlement, he spotted Delia and Danny Limetree, in a company of other East Tinderwick back-woodsers. They'd assembled huts and a teepee, smoke gently issuing from its flapped vent. Farther off, the lean-tos and sheds the Spodosolians had established. Journeyman remembered the "fairy houses" they'd built at the camp. Tiny stone-and-stick palaces, roofed with clumps of moss. If the reluctant forest hippies of East Tinderwick's secret forests had been miniaturized, they'd have been precisely the fairies the children had waited to see come occupy the little villages they'd made ready.

Meanwhile, at the cleared site on the island's promontory, where old quarry slag had been rearranged for Astur's lighthouse project,

the industrious Spodosolians had produced a year's worth of infra-
structure, a new town square.

Impressive, yet looking close, provisional, too. These were lean-
tos, shacks, a campsite. "Glamping"—that was the old name. Renee
and Ernesto stood at the fire with a wide square skillet, grilling egg-
and-cheese-and-spinach sandwiches on chunky biscuits and handing them to all takers. The chickens who'd supplied the eggs ran
loose, among the five or six dogs. Lucius and Jane put themselves
in line for a breakfast, and Journeyman did as well. Ed Waltz and
Dodie Metzger and Nils had just been served and now transported
their egg biscuits back over the rise, where the lighthouse's ragged
upper reaches loomed above the tree line.

Journeyman took his biscuit in hand and went to find his sister.
Maddy knelt inside the communal sleeping shed, ordering rows of
mason-jarred beets and kimchi and brined string beans onto shelves
formed of the lintels and jambs of the unfinished interior walls. Had
Spodosol's winter stores been cleared out? How long would they
harbor on this island?

"Hey," he said.

"Hey," returned Maddy. "Glad you made it." He saw she wore
the claw hammer on her tool belt. She was never without it anymore.

"What needs doing?" he asked.

Maddy turned from the work and gave Journeyman a short,
tight smile. "You might help Dodie and Paulo stack the bonfires.
On the ridge."

"Bonfires? On the ridge?"

"For later." There was nothing unfriendly in how she left him
guessing.

"Ah."

Others had landed, from precincts beyond East Tinderwick.
Mike Raritan's boat had sailed direct from Tinderwick proper, landing twenty minutes or so after Astur's. His passengers included Sophie Thurber, and Edwin Gorse's daughters. The two girls stepped

wide-eyed into the midst of the refugee collective, were fed and given a show of the facilities: the slapdash outhouse, the potable water supply. After eating breakfast they were enlisted scrubbing dishes with Andy the shrink.

Was Drenka still at the library?

One residence had been carpentered to winter through: Eke and Walt's cabin. Astur and Maddy had cast the two for a permanent fate here. The former Cordon men queued for egg biscuits behind the Gorse girls, who stared at the bearded men and were rewarded with kindly smiles. They seemed becalmed. Or was it resigned to their fates? Were Eke and Walt prisoners of this island, or defectors taking asylum?

No, the tower, at the summit of the old cleared quarry path: that too had been built to last. An uncanny sink of labor and resources, of village time, expended in a visionary cause that still eluded Journeyman. Would another French boat appear, to gratify the effort? It seemed as likely as fairies appearing to occupy the William Tell village.

They might themselves be the fairies they'd been waiting for.

62.

RECROSSING, RESCUE, RECON

ASTUR TAPPED JOURNEYMAN ON THE elbow. "Come," she said.

"Where?"

"We need to go back, you and I. We're going to rescue your friend Augustus."

"Maddy said I should help with the firewood."

Astur shook her head. "The fires are prepared. Better you come with me."

Paulo saw them heading down to the rowboat, and offered to join them. He seemed to know Astur's mission—everyone seemed to know more than Journeyman did.

Astur waved him off. "You stay. Sandy can help. We may need the space in the boat."

She rowed them toward the mooring. A wind had risen since their journey out, Astur's oars gently battling the steady rippling waves. Her tacking brought them a view of the tower's height.

"It's almost finished," said Journeyman, fishing.

Astur smiled, but shook her head. "It won't be completed until you add to the effort."

"I don't understand."

"We need you, Sandy. You need only add a single straw."

"Is that an old Somalian aphorism?"

"No, Sandy, it isn't a Somalian aphorism."

Journeyman felt obscurely humiliated. He stared back at the tower. Did it shake and clatter in this rising wind? Or was that only the scaffolding? Perhaps it waited for the stabilizing contribution of his single straw.

They tacked long, away from East Tinderwick, hugging the windward shore. Where did Astur mean to land? Center harbor was too visible, it seemed to Journeyman, if they were to sneak into town in daylight. Another plan he'd wait to have revealed.

"Look," Astur said.

She pointed at the surface. They crossed a sinuous watery field, as if through the wake of an invisible boat. Something churned in the depths. Journeyman spotted a train of bubbles rising from below. They passed above the inching progress of the supercar, along the bay's floor. A wandering abyss, it matched Journeyman's mood. He recalled a cartoon he'd seen, depicting a "Nixon Monument": citizens ringed around a gigantic sinkhole, gazing down. And the sculptor Laird Noteless's catastrophic urban earthwork, the notorious "fjord" he'd excavated into a Harlem hillside, into which New Yorkers had pitched their garbage and sometimes their suicidal bodies.

Suicide: was the Blue Streak even watertight? Todbaum and Theodore Nowlin might be entombed in the mud-depths. Yet the skim was etched with weird waveform. If the supercar was stilled, Journeyman reasoned, it would have been instantly. Not a quarter mile out. Astur tacked them through the water palimpsest, and beyond.

She skirted center harbor. Passing, he strained to make out any sign of activity on Bay Street. Nothing. Was that a figure on horseback, watching through the trees that ringed the playground? Journeyman might be fooling himself. A column of gray smoke rose from the center of town. Impossible to know which street from the distance of the water. A bonfire? Odd in midmorning. The light was perfect, like the day Todbaum had been escorted down their road.

Astur drew them close past the spit concealing them from the harbor's view. She tied up at the country club marina, amid the abandoned sloops that bobbed in wet slip, waiting for summer people who'd never retrieve them. Fair camouflage, though her main sail stood out among the bare masts. They rowed into the club's boathouse.

"This feels like a plan," Journeyman said to Astur.

"That's because it is one."

The butcher waited there. Augustus Cordell. He sat, plainly waiting, huddled beneath a tarp for disguise. Journeyman felt dismayed at the orchestration of so many occurrences outside his grasp. Augustus seemed glad to see him, though. He greeted Journeyman in a stage whisper likely unnecessary against the sound of surf lapping into the boathouse walls. Astur brought the boat near. Augustus handed over heavy bundles of product for Journeyman to heave into the rowboat—lard, bacon, whole fowls, raw cuts in waxcloth. The butcher had been pushing, these last weeks, Journeyman suddenly understood, in advance of this moment. Pigs had died for the retreat to Quarry Island.

He Suddenly Understood. It might be Journeyman's epitaph.

The goods half-submerged the rowboat. Augustus didn't follow them in. "I need to check on Mr. Gorse," he said. "There's fire up at his place."

"I can wait half an hour," said Astur. "No more. I don't want to sail without you, but I will."

"I get the picture," said Augustus.

"I'll go too," Journeyman said.

"Please stay, Sandy. This is my last crossing."

"I'll be okay if I'm left in town. Those people know me." Journeyman meant the Cordon men with whom he'd been transacting on behalf of the peninsula for years now. Whether those would be the same he'd meet in town wasn't certain.

"Perhaps so," said Astur. "But you're needed on the island."

"I'll be back within half an hour," he said. The path to High Street, where Gorse lived, curved up past the library. He'd look for Drenka. Even if Augustus retrieved Gorse and Journeyman could convince Drenka to join them on the island and they were therefore too many for Astur's scull, they weren't too many for her sailboat. Journeyman knew its capacity. He'd row from shore to sailboat a second time himself, if he had to. He could rescue her.

63.

THE FIRE

HIGH STREET WAS EMPTY, BUT it reeked. The telltale fumes of shit-cycles. Did the butcher know this scent? Not likely as well as Journeyman did, from his meetings out on the road.

Yet there was more to the smell. Fire. Smoke still trickled up from the smoldering roof, past the concealing hedge, to the sky. The laurel hadn't kept out anything that mattered. That barricade-like hedge that had been Edwin Gorse's way of setting himself apart from them.

Had this alone been enough to draw the Cordon's attack? The sense of barricade? More likely the Cordon people knew Gorse was often down at the park with Todbaum. Guilt by association. Or they had questions. They'd cornered Gorse and he'd made a stand, Journeyman supposed. That was what Gorse had been looking to do.

The house was one of the oldest in town, built for some ship's captain or quarry owner. Its bones were strong enough to resist collapse, but the flames had licked the paint black where they hadn't eaten the cladding to the bare frame, and they'd eaten most of it. Journeyman tried to remember the true colors and failed.

Augustus found the body. The third scent in the air. Gorse had gotten himself backed into the kitchen, at the rear. He'd died shoved down between the island counter and the sink. A modern kitchen. Dishwasher and microwave, dead relics unremoved. Journeyman's noticing these was surely a symptom of numb dissociation.

Had Gorse no remaining avenue of escape? Or only believed he hadn't? Had they beaten him senseless, before the blaze? Broken his legs? No way to know at a glance, and there wouldn't be an autopsy. Had Gorse refused to cede the house until it was too late? Possibly it was ablaze on several sides. Perhaps the Cordon also felt *the worth of ritual action*. Their way of saying, simply, we were here. We did come. A definite statement in an indefinite time. Would it be their only statement? Or merely their first?

Journeyman touched the butcher's shoulder. "Let's go."

"We should bury him," Augustus said.

"It'll wait. We need to get to the island."

"She won't leave without us."

"She might," Journeyman said. "I want to make another stop, at the library."

Augustus nodded. They left.

64.

GONE

RISKING THEMSELVES IN PLAIN SIGHT, Journeyman and Augustus rattled the library's front doors. Locked. Embarrassed, Journeyman drew the line at shouting Drenka's name. Approaching noon, the town lay vacant around them. Had the Cordon already withdrawn? This didn't seem a bet worth making. The fire on High Street, Journeyman's running shoes encrusted with ash, made silence a portent. Augustus glanced at the tree line, behind it the playground, the town beach, the cloaking woods they'd traveled through, into town. There, Astur waited to salvage them. If they hurried.

"I'll check the back," Journeyman said.

The rear entrance was unlocked. Journeyman stepped inside. Nothing. No sign, no evidence of intrusion. Just the bookish vault she'd made her home.

Augustus had to make Journeyman accept what he'd found, much as Journeyman had needed to rattle the butcher loose at Gorse's. "She's not here."

"Yes."

"So, let's go."

Journeyman mumbled consent.

Drenka's boat, gone too. For months it lay inverted beneath a tarp on the golf course beach. Now, rowing with Astur and the butcher out to Astur's sailboat, that one solitary banner amid the bare masts, Journeyman spotted the tarp. Discarded, flapping in the day's breeze. Was she safe, where she'd gone? Would he ever know? Drenka, her craft, now among the missing things that might never have been there in the first place.

65.

BUBBLE

THEY PASSED OVER IT AGAIN, returning. The roil, the susurrus denoting the action of the Streak as it burrowed through murky bottom-stuff, toward Quarry Island. Had Astur steered them to find it? Had she sought to measure its progress in the time they'd been gone? It had certainly made progress. Yet Astur and Journeyman said nothing. It was their guilty secret, somehow. Augustus sat weeping in the back of the sailboat. Butchery hadn't prepared him. One never knew.

As they tacked past the zone of disgruntled water, a single large bubble rose, to burst with an audible *plop* on the surface. As though the deep-hidden supercar had farted. This, too, they politely left unremarked.

IV.

YET ANOTHER ARREST

66.

THE CIRCLE OF THE KNOWN

THE THING MOVING UNSEEN THROUGH torrents of mud was also a kind of clock, ticking. The sun had gone behind the clouds now. It marked the afternoon's swift passage whether one looked up to see, or not. Beneath it the island had an anthill's intensity, seething yet methodical. Unfrantic. Each person tracked to a purpose, some obscurer than others. Food stacked to the rafters of the sleeping shed. A repurposed stone well, into which the meat and cider had been lowered, on oiled ropes, to reside in the deep cool.

Bonfires built yet unlit, strategically arranged. Waiting.

The machine wouldn't arrive until dark. This time of year, four thirty in the afternoon. No matter how mild the air.

Just one fire was lit, in the center of the camp, far from the tower. Jane and Lucius placed bowls of some savory mash in the hands of any who approached. There, Journeyman's sister and her lover sat talking to a couple of the newest arrivals, Augustus among them. Augustus still wept. He'd come into the circle and told what he'd seen, the scorched remains. Was Journeyman numbed? Yes. Numbed and in wonder and wondering. Jane put a bowl into his hands. It held beans and spinach and tomato. Journeyman felt starved after the terrors and disappointments of town. The peninsula now under a cloud of occupation. Journeyman in a vision beheld the Arrest entire. Or anyway felt he did. The Arrest obliterated assumptions. It shrank the world, the circle of the known. This place, the island to which they'd fallen back, was the consoling world yet further shrunken. Augustus still wept. The butcher hadn't been a butcher, before. He'd been a manager and teller in Tinderwick's branch of one of Maine's regional banks.

The talk changed again. Maddy spoke as though offering a tour of the island. "It's bedrock, there's no tunneling through," she said. "And the fir stand is too dense. No way that thing can crawl up the leeside beach."

"So?" This was Lucius.

"So he'll circle the island and feel his way up the quarry path. There's no back door. He does that or keeps on."

"Him and Theodore Nowlin," Journeyman pointed out, eager to be included. It was the only thing he knew. "I saw them last night, before they embarked."

"Is someone watching the beach?" Lucius asked, ignoring Journeyman.

"We'll hear it coming," said Astur.

"So, what's the plan here?" Journeyman asked. "And does everyone know it except me?"

Was it Journeyman's imagination? Did all at the fire turn to him? Did some smile? Was Journeyman merely the comic relief in this story? He sat with his bowl on an upright section of tree trunk. His sister sat beside him. Ed Waltz came nearer, and put his hands on Journeyman's shoulders from behind. Ed had been crying too.

"Eat," Maddy said.

"Yes."

"You'll need your strength for later."

Journeyman felt the pressure of their averted gazes. "I get it now," he said to his sister. "The whole deal with this island."

"What is the whole deal with this island?"

"You're throwing me that surprise party I always said I never wanted."

"I knew you'd guess, Sandy."

67.

ANOTHER ARREST, PART 1

IT BEGAN FOR JOURNEYMAN WITH a sunset walk, led by Astur. The island, clotted with scraped bluffs, stands of pine, and bunkerlike mounds of quarry slag, couldn't be circumnavigated. But it was riddled with trails. The oldest, boot-engraved in granite dust a century ago. The newest, grass or bramble flattened in recent weeks. Astur seemed intent on walking them all in the magic-hour evening.

They strolled down to the old landing for the quarry barges. The predicted spot for Todbaum's arrival. The wide beach lay ringed with unlit bonfires, as if prepared for some ceremony. This was the clearing where the assemblage Journeyman thought of as the crab claw had been welded together, yet now the thing wasn't in evidence. How did it vanish? Journeyman asked Astur. She guided him to the surf's edge. The tidemark was at two-thirds on the rocks, still coming in. Astur pointed. Amid the disguising rockweed fronds the claw tips were just discernible, protruding from the muck in which the vast apparatus had been sunk, presumably at low tide.

Journeyman didn't ask more.

They climbed to the tower that rose through the trees. Dodie Metzger stood nearly at its top, disassembling the flat platform on

which she stood, lowering planks by rope and pulley. At the foot
Paulo untied the planks and shoved them aside in a heap. Journeyman realized he'd never distinguished tower from scaffolding. That
husk now mostly stripped away, twin tensile cables, thick as arms,
lay exposed. They ran on brackets down the tower's ocean face, then
fed through winches low to the ground, south through the impass-
able woods. The winches and cable were boatyard stuff. Ed Waltz's
work before the Arrest had been to winter the large summer boats,
dragging them in and out of the water. Ed was the winchman, then.
Now again.

Another old path snaked to the cliffs. Astur led. The moon was
risen, two-thirds, like the tide. The cables led to this spot. They'd
been bolted through the vast weatherworn, birdshit-splattered granite block that had been so long abandoned, staring off to sea. Then
secured on the block's far side by a new steel plate. The cliff where
the block sat had been worked too, strategically undermined, the
ground beneath it broken. The granite hunk now jutted over the
precipice, threatening to tumble into the sea, or at least to the thin
pebble beach that lay below.

Journeyman smelled steel shavings, rotting mussel shells sea-
birds had smashed on the granite block's roof, thyme wafting from
underfoot.

The moon large enough to hold his thoughts.

Journeyman stepped to the edge. Nothing below apart from an
overturned rowboat, dragged up just above the tide line.

The same rowboat?

68.

A PICTURE

WEEKS LATER JOURNEYMAN TRIMMED TWO more pictures out of library books. This reminded him of the tower.

69.

ANOTHER ARREST, PART 2

THE MOON CLIMBED AND SHRANK. Lucius brewed morning tea on the remains of the central campfire—he wouldn't let anyone else make it; he was fed up with their bad cooking, here at the end of the world. No fires were lit, on this darkening island. They waited. Someone produced a guitar. There was always a guitar. The coffee went around, and cake too. There was always cake, in foil that had been painstakingly rinsed and dried a hundred times. Some stood on the beach watching the sea glitter. Ed futzed at the winches. As the dark fell their eyes adjusted. Soon it was evident they had watchers on that other shore. New occupants of Founder's Park, Cordon people. They'd lit fires of their own. Presumably stood watching, looking out as those on Quarry Island looked out. They'd have read the signs, the tread marks grinding into the water. The Blue Streak was strung between them, on its way. But nearer to the island now. Quite near the island.

In the park, two fires, one bigger than the other. One grew and grew and then the roof lit, revealing the shape. The whole frame erupted. They'd torched the gazebo.

Down by the water Augustus went on quietly talking with others about Edwin Gorse, about what he and Journeyman had seen in the charred kitchen.

They spotted the disturbance in the water. The churning in the field of moonglint. As if a pot of spaghetti had come to boil beneath the waves. A seething, tracked by wheeling black birds. Shouldn't it be seagulls, not crows? Crows were perhaps Todbaum's special envoy. They flapped off overhead into the trees. The water's dancing reflections gave way to the lifting glow. The bald pale lamp seeping up from the floor of the harbor, a kind of reply to the moon.

Haloed within, two figures riding. Mr. Toad in his motorcar, and, bent over his shoulder, the idiot-Gandalf, Nowlin. *Sit down*, Journeyman begged Nowlin silently, in the instant before the trap was sprung. He was an old man, after all.

The Blue Streak sought purchase on the dry shore, treads shrieking from beneath the sucking sand. At that instant, the halves of the trap emerged. The claws, sprung by the supercar's weight. Robotic pincers festooned with seaweed and black clay, stinking of salt rot; these rose along either side of Todbaum's vehicle, surrounding it. Less a crab claw than a kind of Venus flytrap. Not particularly swift, but neither was the Blue Streak, not at this vulnerable moment, its Darwinian crawl from sea to land. The halves clamped around the Streak's sides, scraping and grinding as they secured themselves around its treads and chassis. The four topmost fingers of the trap rose as far as the glass dome, met there, and intertwined. The clutching fingers eerily underlit. *Here is the church, here is the steeple. Open the doors, and see all the people.*

Journeyman readied himself for the dome to be crushed like an eggshell. For Todbaum and Nowlin to ooze forth like yolks. No. It held without shattering. Journeyman lost sight of the men inside. Did they cower on the floor? Or had they moved into the hidden parts of the supercar: engine room, bunk, toilet?

The Streak's treads seized up in the trap's grip. Though innumerable small valves and tubes and doodads that ran along the outside surface of the supercar were crushed by the bite of the trap, the integrity of the thing was uncompromised. The cockpit un-shattered. Yet the thing calmed. Its engines faded to a whine, barely audible over the surf and the roaring of blood in Journeyman's ears. The two machines—slick doomsday craft, grimy artisanal nemesis—had married into one impossible object.

The quiet lasted barely a minute before it was drowned in the grinding and screeching, from high on the hill, of Ed Waltz's ma-chine. The winches turned and the twin cables revealed themselves from beneath the sand as they leapt to tautness. They not only reached from the tower to the titanic block on the far cliff. They also extended under the beach and into the sea, anchored to the trap. The whole island was a machine, Journeyman saw now. Cantilevered from claw to tower to perching ballast of granite. Tick by tick, the ancient winches that had hauled boats from the sea now heaved the knuckled welter of claw-and-car past the high-surf mark, onto the high beach where they'd arrayed themselves. Hauled it into their midst, where it was licked with reflected flame.

Maddy had been igniting the bonfires. Renee and Ernesto and Dodie and Nils and Andy the shrink and Jane and Lucius were with her, bearing shovels and rakes. Journeyman began to feel he understood, if only in part. The dry wood sprang rapidly to blaz-ing. With shovels and rakes, those on the beach tipped and shoved the fresh orange coals to situate beneath the arms of the apparatus, the claw trap, the vise in which the supercar remained held, tipped slightly upward, immobilized entirely. What better conductor of the woodfire's heat than that bare rusted iron? Journeyman thought of *the worth of ritual action* and wondered at the words. As though for a time words had been banished even from rising into mind. No one had spoken, it seemed to Journeyman, since the gazebo had burned, so many fires ago. At a glance that site lay dark. Even then, had words been uttered? Or just murmurs?

But there was one talker here on the island among them. He recommenced his barbaric yawp now, over the Blue Streak's trumpet-like speaker.

"I'll hand it to you, Maddy, I really did get my dick entangled in your IUD here. Only I've seen the specs on the Streak, and I'm here to tell you: the melting point of this hafnium-carbon alloy is something like three-K Celsius. Nothing you're liable to approach with your driftwood and shit, though it's a real pretty fireworks show."

The winches were halted, for now. The Streak's treads unflailing against their captivity. Had they been stilled by the claw's hold? Or had Todbaum chosen to conserve his energies for some next struggle or stratagem? His voice went silent too. The only sound, the crackle and hiss of the flames massed around the caged supercar. That and the waves lapping. Then Maddy stepped up and spoke in a voice loud enough to be heard where Journeyman stood. He knew the Blue Streak had microphones to convey it into Todbaum's cockpit too.

"Let Nowlin come down."

"Nice try!" barked Todbaum through the speaker. "Ted's my wingman. Me and him have places to be and people to go. You lost your chance to team up, Madeleine. We'll write you a postcard."

"Send him down, we'll scatter the fire."

"I don't give a crap about the fire, that's what I'm trying to say. I'll send him down when you disengage the Jaws of Life here."

Journeyman saw Maddy gesture then to those who fed dry wood to the fires. The supercar nearly engulfed in showering sparks as the fuel ignited. Within shroud of smoke and flame the machine glowed, unholy with radiation, though Journeyman couldn't make out the human forms within the cockpit. How could Nowlin entrust himself to the ladder, if Todbaum were to open the hatch? The Streak's exterior would be white-hot.

"I get it now," said Todbaum. "This is your idea of a collaboration. You're putting on this Kabuki episode for the gang on the mainland. They need to see you gave it a try. It's a good show, Maddy, maybe a great show. If you do their dirty work for them, maybe everything goes back the way it was, hunky-dory, weekly delivery of duck eggs and kale puttanesca in mason jars. Maybe it doesn't matter whether I croak or not, huh?"

Maddy didn't answer. The fires rose. Those on the beach stood back, a semicircle of shining faces. A few tended the fires. Eke and Walt had appeared and were among those working with great zeal with rakes to push the coals nearer, beneath the armature and treads.

"This thing was built to withstand worse than your paleo-guerrilla moves. I'll be sipping martinis while you torch this fucking island to the bedrock."

Across the water, the park lay silent. Todbaum might be right about that much: they'd be watching them now.

"Actually, I take it back. I'm looking at the dashboard indicator, congrats, you're on the brink of inducing a core meltdown in my reactor. I'm about to go all Chernobyl on your ass. What a way to go out, for a bunch of granola-heads. I dunno if the blast'll be enough to actually take out the Cordon too, or just poison the topsoil for a hundred-mile radius. Guess it amounts to the same thing."

Could Todbaum induce a catastrophe out of sheer petulance? Did the supercar's controls include autodestruct? Should the Spodo-solians bet their island refuge on the Last American's nonsuicidality? Journeyman's thoughts drifted then, from the arrangement in steel and sand and fire that lay before him, to that life now vanished outside of the time-smashing, irrelevancy-besotted machine that was his head.

He and Todbaum had once invaded a party at one of the great despised fraternities, Delta Kappa Epsilon. After liberating an un-guarded foil packet of cocaine from a desktop, they'd locked themselves in the fraternity's attic, to snort it. The frat brothers came in numbers to the attic's door, bellowing for them to come out. Todbaum drew a Bic lighter from his pocket and flicked it against an overhead smoke detector and the building erupted in sirens. Campus security and the fire department came and freed Journeyman and Todbaum from the attic, frog-marching them past the outraged frat boys. A week later the two were tried by a student counsel grievance committee, given academic probation.

"Which hill do you want to die on?"—another of Todbaum's favorite sayings. By crawling underwater from the park he'd opted for arrest by Maddy, instead of the Cordon. Why not? Todbaum had crossed the Arrestlands to keep alive a story in his head. Now, on an island at the end of land and time, the hunter had been captured by the game. What did it mean to Todbaum, to deliver the crisis of himself into Maddy's hands? For Todbaum the higher cause might be to keep from dying on the hill of yourself.

Journeyman's thoughts seemed as ill-fitted as those oceangoing crows. Like the crows, they hovered over Todbaum.

He was startled back to the proceedings on the beach. Todbaum had dilated the porthole and freed Theodore Nowlin. Eke and Walt kicked and raked away the chunks of fire nearest to the Blue Streak and stepped up to help him down from the ladder. Was it banishment, or had Nowlin changed his mind, bargained for escape? With Eke and Walt's guidance, the tall man vaulted free, then staggered a ways from the flame-licked supercar, to end on his knees in the sand. He'd survived both the ocean tunneling and being roasted in the cockpit, not the gentlest ticket to the island. He'd rejoined them now, woken from his dream of returning. Quarry Island had been far enough to go, after all. Todbaum was going no farther.

Maddy and Astur and others rushed to damp the flames, to smother the coals with garlands of wet seaweed. Hiss and steam covered the beach as the fires quickly sputtered, became wreckage, beach crap. The moon's light again prevailed. That, and the cockpit's glow. The Streak lay like an egg cradled in a fox's mouth. No one inside but Todbaum. Journeyman thought he saw him, shrouded in steam and light. The winches groaned again to life, then began a steady clanking as they ratcheted the trap and its contents inch by inch up the beach. Toward the quarry path. Toward the tower.

70.

DRENKA WAS THERE

JOURNEYMAN SPOTTED DRENKA THEN, AS they trudged silently up the dark path behind the shrieking, grinding mass. When she'd joined their company he couldn't know. But it was her rowboat parked below the cliff. She saw him see her and she almost smiled, Journeyman could have sworn it.

71.

LAST STORIES

TODBAUM RAILED THROUGH HIS PROGRESS uphill, toward the tower. Difficult to make him out over the effort of the device, the scrape of metal and stone. His amplified voice became part of that roar. By the time the winches quit, having dragged the claw-bound supercar to a point of rest at the tower's foot, Todbaum had gone into a bargaining phase. Now he entreated not to Maddy, but to anyone who'd listen.

"Who wants coffee? How long's it been for you poor sonsabitches?"

No one spoke.

"Pity. We could get a nice thing going on this island if you'd just crown me King Turd. Speaking of which, you got working shitholes here? 'Cause I feature immaculate facilities; you can ask Nowlin if you want. Anyone requiring an 'interlude,' as my mom used to call it, is welcome aboard."

Theodore Nowlin had staggered up the incline, still supported by Eke and Walt. Todbaum's old company in the park, Journeyman noted.

"The more the merrier, as you know, it's the shit that keeps the show running."

Ed Waltz and Dodie Metzger and Nils and Renee and Ernesto busily engaged the undercarriage of the crab to the armature of the tower. It was a kind of train track, Journeyman saw. A railroad pointed to the sky.

"I see what you're getting at here. It's in a spirit I endorse, believe me—every dollar is on the screen! But if you think I'm going to *engage thruster rockets* or some such shit to complete the picture, you got another thing coming. I can't for the life of me see how you're closing this deal."

Journeyman saw it. At last, he saw it. This whole island converted to a gigantic kit for raising Todbaum and the Blue Streak to the top of the tower. Todbaum wouldn't know of the closer, the enormous granite chunk balanced perilously on the south cliffs, the ballast to which he was now shackled.

"Ah . . . so . . . you're probably wondering why I've gathered you here today. *God, I still love that joke!* So, yeah, let's not overlook in our artisanal zeal the common enemy we're facing here, people! Them that chased us off the mainland, amiright? In any final battle scenario you quaint farm folk are gonna need my odious retro-tech. This exoskeleton of mine works like a rolling people-crusher kind of gizmo, it's meant to stay on the road . . . Maybe if you want to put someone on top of a tower it ought to be one of your vegan chefs, to dump a cauldron of piping-hot miso chowder with lemongrass on their heads, huh?"

Journeyman savored his faceless role inside whatever it was they consisted of now: anonymizing collective, silent mob. Naturally, then, Todbaum singled him out.

"Sandman!"

Why should Journeyman believe himself invisible? The Blue Streak's dashboard, lined with tiny monitors, made a three-sixty view of its surroundings. The high moon and the supercar's glow provided the lighting. Todbaum had sunk into his captain's chair, a blot in the radiance.

"Well, *mon petit frère*, you turned the tables. So, what's your play?"

Maddy avoided Journeyman's gaze, gave no clue. Journeyman was stirred by a smell. Ed Waltz's winches and pulleys, lathered in pig grease. It wafted out with a burnt tinge as the cables labored at the supercar's weight. For weeks Journeyman had obediently delivered the unrefined lard to the boatworks, never thinking to ask its purpose. The communal machine working around him, leaving him oblivious. Journeyman felt as though he were not here on the ground but trapped in the cockpit with Todbaum. That, like Nowlin, he needed to be bargained free.

"What, you can't come up with a line? You never did write the villains too great, Sanderton. You're a sidekick, you write what you know."

The Spodosolians began to move, in silence, following the cables where they led into the trees. Drenka moved in the same direction, a little apart from the group. Not having yet joined or enlisted herself to anything. No one appeared to question her witnessing role among them on the island, whether it puzzled them or not. Journeyman wanted to call to her, but didn't.

"So now you found your way to a murder party at world's end. Elegant scheme. Blow me up like a fireworks, make it visible from shore, play for both teams. Do a good murder, Sandy."

Journeyman heard himself speak. "Nobody's doing a murder, Peter."

"What do you think this inverted piñata of doom is for? You're offing me in fucking Sensurround. I'm proud of what I taught you, Sandy. What's that joke? How did the cadaver heckle the comedian? *I died onstage, like you.* Hey, where you going? I say something wrong?"

Astur started for the cliff. Nils too, and Renee and Ernesto, their effort at the winch concluded. Only Ed and Dodie remained stationed at the tower's bacon-stinky mechanism, to monitor the works. Maddy waited for Journeyman, though shirking his gaze. Moon sped behind cloud, the tower's summit now barely visible. Now only pale glaring dome. That egg, that rheumy eye. Todbaum's dark bulk its rotten yolk or pupil. Scent of scorched lard and crushed thyme, mingled in air of salt rot, raked seaweed, the supercar's garlands. Faint lapping of waves, squeak of the trap, Todbaum's voice.

"Come back and talk, you silent fucking pissants. You peasants, you posse. You pussies. You're going to miss me. I swear if you just say something I'll shut the fuck up and listen. I'm just talking to hear myself think. How do you think I made it all this way? I have to talk on drives, man, you know? I have to keep my thoughts outside my head in this motherfucker. I should never have kicked Pittsburgh out of the car; she had some motherfucking balls on her, that one. Listen to that hollow fucking ringing, it's like the sound of one hand clapping, worst sound in the world. You need me, I'm your sole survivor. None of you know shit about what's out there. I came all this way. None of you fucking know. None of you had anything to fucking survive before I came along. You fucking need me."

"Come out," Journeyman said. He heard in himself again a gentle undertow of the police. *Please exit the vehicle.*

"You're fucking kidding me."

"Why not? They'll find a job for you to do."

"A job?"

"They even found a job for me," Journeyman joked.

"I have a fucking job. I'm your storyteller. I'm your story."

"Tell your story on the ground."

"No." Maddy stepped into the radiant circle, the field of distortion.

"No what?"

"Sandy's mistaken. We don't have a job for you."

"There you go, Sandman, like I said. A murder party."

"This island is your place now," said Maddy, almost absently.

"Island of the fuckwads! Who lives here, Eke and Ekette? Eating pickled dandelions? No thank you very fucking kindly! I live in supreme splendor, I live in the lap of fucking luxury. I think I got a few jars of beluga in the back of the fridge. I definitely got the last working cache of hentai anime porn in the known galaxy. Ever fuck a cartoon, Sandy? Better than the real thing, though I doubt you've got a point of comparison, these days. I'm still breathing recirculated air trapped here from Malibu Beach, wouldn't trade it for the world. The Pacific, now that is a real fucking ocean, the blue fucking horizon, none of this *E. coli*, red-tide, a-daughter-of-the-*Mayflower*-once-cut-her-foot-on-this-very-barnacle shit. Give me the Pacific any day. I should have stayed home. But I'll go down with the fucking ship, yessir, *shantih, shantih, shantih*."

Did the words suggest finality? Journeyman should have known better than to suspect Todbaum, ever, of finality. Todbaum's tone changed, then, rose out of the depths of his barrel chest, high into his mouth or sinuses. He whined, yes. But also he was doing one of his voices. "I don't wanna die." It turned into a kind of incantation, though the words were never the same twice. "I don't wanna die up there. I don't wanna go up there. Don't send me up there to die. Don't wanna go up the murder tower. Don't wanna get murdered. Don't murder me up the tower. I don't *wanna* go up there."

Journeyman stood dumbstruck. Maddy knelt, palm resting on her holstered hammer, to confer in a whisper with Ed and Dodie. Todbaum's voice filled Journeyman's head. Journeyman recognized it now, the voice. Todbaum's Sandy Duplessis impression. Unmistakable, once Journeyman allowed himself to hear. "Don't *make* me go up there. Don't make me. No go up there. No murder up tower. No no mamma. No mamma no murder no tower. I don't wanna wanna. Don't wanna wanna do it. I didn't didn't do it. I didn't do whatcha say. I never never said it. I never did do do it. I didn't done it nohow. I didn't doo doo. Didda doo doo poo poo."

Maddy tugged Journeyman by the hand to shatter the spell of Todbaum's voice. They were back on Rehoboth, Journeyman imagined.

"Maddy?"

"Yes?"

"Is this revenge?"

"Revenge for what?"

"What Peter did, in the Starlet. When you came to visit."

"I don't care what he did in the Starlet, Sandy. You're the only one who even remembers."

"So why does he have to die?"

"He doesn't have to die, his car does. Todbaum just has to stay on the island, where Eke and Walt can watch him."

"Because of what he did coming across? The people he killed?"

"Because he's a ripple in the field."

"He thinks you're the author of the Arrest, you know. Because of *Yet Another World*. He thinks one half of the story is trying to win."

"I'm not interested in that," said Maddy firmly.

"It's not personal," Journeyman suggested.

"Not for me. Maybe for you."

"Why for me?"

"It's your voice he's putting on, you know. All the nonsense shit. Goo goo gaga, oinka doinka doo."

Todbaum's abject catechism went on, broadcast to the ocean fog, the moon's veil, now grown tattered. His voice rose into the starry void. "No no murder mamma don't wanna no go dojo poo poo tower up go wanna go homo lobrow no soap radio no no low blow no glow hobo ho ho don't wanna wanna wanna go go—"

Maddy nodded her chin at the path the others had followed. Tugged Journeyman's hand again. Journeyman allowed himself to be led this way. Guided. To the ocean cliffs. To next occasions.

"Sandy?" Todbaum called out.

Maddy put one finger to her lips. She stepped onto the path. Journeyman followed.

"I hope you don't imagine you're getting a percentage of gross on this deal."

72.

ANOTHER ARREST, PART 3

MOON AND STARS WHIRRED THROUGH black awning, racing them to the cliffside. The ceremony's conclusion was underway. Paulo and Ernesto and Andy labored with picks and crowbars, with chisels and wedges, undermining the counterweight stone, to which the cables were strung taut, as if securing moon to earth. Chunks of stone prized loose, exposing roots that dangled over the water. The granite block might just be a hair's breadth, a hair trigger, from tumbling now, it looked to Journeyman.

Drenka stood at the edge of the group, half in, half out. With her there, hovering, Edwin Gorse's daughters. Journeyman wondered what those girls had been told. Whether they'd been told. By whom.

Maddy tended Journeyman, guided him, helped him to understand what his work was to be here. She passed him her claw hammer. A wedge had been placed at the base of the stone block. Cliff, stone and soil, sodden to mud by ocean water siphoned up from the beach below. A few blows to make it all topple off into the sea. These few blows had been saved for Journeyman. Never the author, he was sometimes given last word. Maddy placed her hands against the backs of Journeyman's, her fingers through his fingers around the hammer's handle. Then released him to do the work himself, to strike. Journeyman struck. And again. It took every piece of his strength, but the wedge bit deeper. Mud and gravel shuddered, sucked, liquefied, gave way. The block tipped. He struck again; the cliff's face crumbled, the block fell roaring into the surf, the imprisoned supercar ascending howling on larded cables to take its place as the tower's head, a sunflower weary with time. A glimmering oracle to answer the moon. Beacon of warning to all future French boats. The hammer fell from Journeyman's hands.

All turned to behold it. At last.

Astur's lighthouse.

73.

ONE MORE PICTURE FOR THE FILES

V.

AFTERMATH

74.

BREAKFAST

BY MORNING THE PLUMES OF smoke had died. The beach fires gone cold, rinsed over at high tide. Those set by the Cordon, the two at Founder's Park, now layered in dew. The remains of Edwin Gorse's house too, when they reached it later. Settled to ash and cinder.

Lucius had taken command of the island's last, the cook fire. He ladled out bowls of hot grains and compote and they wandered to the beach at low tide and breakfasted in the bright cold morning. A few went down to boats, then a few more. Journeyman sighted Drenka but didn't approach. She sat eating with Augustus. Journeyman at first felt jealous. But Drenka and the butcher sat with Gorse's daughters and Journeyman saw the girls had been told about their father. Drenka sat close with them. Journeyman kept his distance, instead found his way to Astur's boat for the crossing.

75.

CYNTHIA
PITCHINGS'S ACCOUNT

WHEN THEY APPEARED BEFORE HER she'd fed them. That was what Spodosol did, after all. The farm was for growing and feeding. The people of the Cordon when they finally came were nothing if not hungry. So Cynthia had laid out a table full of food and drink.

Spodosol's was a good, long table, wooden and scarred by smokes laid on its edges and by the rings of cast-iron skillets and cooking pots set down without protection. They sat there now, listening to Cynthia Pitchings's account. Journeyman had helped Astur secure the boat, then walked with her past the park with its ravaged gazebo, down the path to Spodosol. They'd come to see how Spodosol had fared through the night. They sat drinking cider, and Cynthia Pitchings related what had gone on when the Cordon had come.

Cynthia had fed them, then said they should go home. There were no more boats. There would be no more crossings. The persons they sought—the person, the one—was on Quarry Island. He wasn't coming back. They could go confirm it themselves if they liked, but it was unnecessary. Needless. The person was being contained. Arrested. He'd been entrusted to their vigilance, hadn't he, at the start? Now was accounted for by their community, in their manner. It might not be the Cordon's, but it should be enough. They should eat and be content and go home. We all had homes to go to, or nearly all. They ought to keep this blessing in mind.

Had the Cordon people by the end of Cynthia Pitchings's feeding and lecture apologized? Not that, no. They were not people of apology. Had they felt chagrined? Perhaps so.

She'd fed the Cordon, and now she fed the islanders, for they were again hungry. Possibly they'd never stop eating. Hot loaves were just coming out and Cynthia and Astur went into the cellars and brought out the good cheeses and the jars of fruit, the rhubarb chutney and pickled corn. At first Journeyman was confused by the profusion: hadn't the stores been evacuated to Quarry Island?

Foolish. He'd been so impressed at a single shed crammed full of mason jars. The Farm had much deeper reserves. What had been ferried to Quarry Island was a winter's share for those who'd go on living on Quarry Island. Eke, and Walt, and Peter Todbaum. Plus a little more, to last the evacuees through the—retreat. Stand? Whatever it should be called. The long day and night of Todbaum's capture and elevation. The amount shifted from Spodosol's cellars to the island was a fraction. The cellars held so much more.

In fact, Cynthia explained she'd sent the Cordon visitors home laden with goods. Treats, as though they'd been obedient dogs. They nearly were dogs, under her hand. Her generosity helped the Cordon people rationalize coming in such numbers: They'd carried back a winter's supply. Wouldn't need to visit again so soon. This turned out true. Journeyman didn't resume handing off goods at the North Grange for several weeks.

Time enough to forget the burning.

Time enough it might seem the tower had always been with them.

Time enough to bury the dead.

76.

THE NOTE

IT HAD BEEN JOURNEYMAN'S FATE to go with Augustus into the Alamo of Edwin Gorse's burnt kitchen. It was his fate also to find Jerome Kormentz's body, alone. No one else had thought of Kormentz. This had been the purpose of his placement at the lake, after all: out of sight, out of mind. Journeyman visited the second morning after the return from the island. Early, in the cold glare. No one followed. No crows in the trees. No one would have known if Journeyman hadn't gone.

They'd cut Kormentz down and placed him in a chair at his kitchen table. Journeyman suspected they'd had to set the table back in place—that Kormentz had used it to climb to the rafter, then kicked it from under his feet. The chair wouldn't have been high enough. The rope still lay around his neck. Journeyman thought they'd wanted whoever discovered Kormentz to see and understand.

The room was very cold. Kormentz had laid a fire, but never started it. Journeyman thought he might, before he walked back to town.

The note, a single folded sheet, lay on the table. Journeyman first imagined it would be in Kormentz's hand. Though this was impossible, if his guess about the table's overturning was correct. It wasn't in Kormentz's hand. It wasn't signed, but it didn't need to be—it spoke for those who'd found him first. Though he could have no proof, Journeyman believed the note.

WE DID NOT MAKE HIM DO IT. HE WAS LIKE THIS WHEN WE GOT UP TO THE HOUSE.

Kormentz had likely hanged himself the moment he heard them coming down his road. The act, an I-told-you-so. A vote in favor of *the worth of ritual action.*

Two lives lost, then, in the Cordon's occupation. Two lives and one house. And a gazebo. Gorse's and Kormentz's deaths rhymed: a suicidal murder, a murderish suicide. Both a form of self-fulfilling assertion. Gorse proved the Cordon were dangerous by dying at their hand, Kormentz that they'd come for him by dying at his own.

Yet Journeyman wondered. Had the discovery of Kormentz's cooling shit-stained body spooked the invaders? The note suggested their reluctance to be implicated in murder. Maybe Kormentz and Gorse had in dying saved the towns. The needlessness of their deaths serving as an admonition to the Cordon: You can't control these people. Stupid-ass hippies might start dying on you right and left. Perhaps it was this that froze the invaders at the shore, or turned them from Spodosol's table.

If so, they'd saved not only Tinderwick but Todbaum.

Journeyman buried the note with Kormentz in the soft bank at the edge of the Lake of Tiredness. No need to light the fire. The digging work warmed him for the walk back to town.

77.

CITADEL OR PRISON?

THE DAYS AFTER TODBAUM'S ASCENSION, Drenka busied herself with Gorse's daughters, so suddenly orphaned and without a home.

Few had gotten to know the girls, thanks to the anxious quarantine their father held around his house. Did Drenka feel that gave them something in common, enough to make them her responsibility? In any case, Raina and Davida moved into the library with her. As if Drenka had found her purpose, a large one, all at once. It hardly punctured her own air of remove. Gorse had protected the girls—now Drenka took up the task. The windows to the library remained shuttered. Drenka's appearances remained fleeting. Caring for the orphaned girls gave her ambivalence a retroactive air of necessity.

Journeyman, as was his responsibility, delivered food for the three of them. Drenka still wouldn't let Journeyman through the door, but after a week or so he managed a question.

"Can we . . . visit sometime?"

"I don't know. Maybe, later."

"Later tonight?"

"Uh-uh. The girls need me."

He returned with fresh bread and sausages, the first sausages since the night on Quarry Island. Drenka accepted the package. When Journeyman suggested he come inside, she shook her head. "They're reading," she said. "I'll walk with you instead. Down by the water."

"That's good."

"I saw you on the island," Drenka said, once they stood in the overgrown lawn sloping behind the hospital.

"I saw you too."

"You knew the man in the car."

"Yes. Peter Todbaum."

"He was your friend."

"Once, I guess."

"But your sister hates him."

"Yes," Journeyman admitted. "I guess she does."

"I want you to tell me why he came here. And why he had to go—up there."

"It's a long story."

"You're a writer, I heard."

"I was."

"Take some notes. You have plenty of time."

"And then we can hang out?"

"We'll see. First, I'm going to help these girls get their heads screwed on right."

She told him why she lived as she did, among them and not. In the library. When she'd first appeared, Augustus and Maddy had each come calling, to ascertain her purposes. To offer welcome, and perhaps a job. A role. Drenka held them at arm's length. "I'd lived in a place a lot like Spodosol, in Lincolnville," she said. "A good organic farm, at first. Seemed like a place I could stay. It went bad in a hurry."

"Bad how?"

"Just bullshit power games. Little tin dictator types, but the passive-aggressive variety. Nothing I could work with, so I came here."

"By rowboat?"

"Once I got to the coast, yeah. I had to get around the Cordon people."

Journeyman thought of Todbaum. This might be all they wanted from him, apart from espresso: persuasive testimony from outside. Drenka had lurked, through those long weeks they'd listened and despaired over Todbaum's lies. What if she could answer the simple questions: Was their peninsula a prison or a citadel? Did the Cordon exaggerate the dangers outside? Were the towns under protection from nightmares, from raiders seeking their food and shelter? Or were they the Cordon's captives, held for their farming and sausage-making, their pickles and preserves?

Yet Drenka demurred. "Lincolnville was sort of like here," she said. "Only more fucked-up."

"But what was outside Lincolnville?"

She shrugged. "Other stuff. I came here when I got sick of it there. I only know what I know."

Journeyman confessed how in the days before the island he'd entertained an elaborate theory. When Todbaum described his traveling companion, the woman he'd nicknamed Pittsburgh, Journeyman imagined, with fascinated horror, that Drenka *was* Pittsburgh.

Who even knew if Pittsburgh even existed? In Todbaum's account he'd expelled the woman from the supercar at the outskirts of New York. In Journeyman's fantasy, during the trip together she'd learned of Todbaum's plans and come to warn them. Even to take revenge. At the peak of paranoia, Journeyman imagined that Drenka had met secretly with Maddy and Astur, to plan the ceremony. The trap, the lighthouse.

Drenka only laughed.

"I never met your friend. I certainly never would have gotten into his car."

"I see that now."

"You thought I rowed up the coast from New York City?"

Journeyman was embarrassed. "I didn't think about that part of it."

"I rowed from Lincolnville Beach. Even that nearly killed me."

"Of course."

"Tell the truth in what you write," she said then.

"I'm afraid," said Journeyman.

"Afraid of what?"

"That I'll arouse your contempt."

"I can't afford contempt. Contempt is too expensive nowadays. I'm just careful."

"Careful?"

"Of places like this. All the fucking drama. You and your crazy sister, her and her organic army. You scare me. But I don't have contempt for you, or anyone."

"Afraid you won't like me, then."

"Liking you might be even more expensive. I'll see you later, Mr. Duplessis."

78.

JOURNEYMAN TIME
AVERAGED HIMSELF

THE ARREST HADN'T ABOLISHED THE regime of mirrors, the way it had those of gasoline and pixels. Mirrored surfaces were everywhere, even for those like Journeyman who'd excluded them from the walls of their homes. The windows of the library and other buildings, caught at the right angle of sunlight. Or of a firelit interior, at night. The rearviews of junked cars. A group of local kids had snapped a number of these off and mounted them high on the rocky beach above Founder's Park, to form a glinting array. Like the old fields of signal-seeking SETI satellite dishes, these beckoned to who-knew-who, to imaginary aircraft.

Journeyman indulged in deliberate Time Averaging. An inquiry into the lurking matter of the self. He did it from Astur's boat. Gliding into a mooring, moments before reaching out with a docking line. The water wasn't always smooth, but often enough. Journeyman puzzled on his own face. Like Narcissus, though with results less flattering. Gazing into those depths, Journeyman thought also of the Arthurian Lady of the Lake. No one, he was certain, would hand him a sword.

79.

THOSE BIRDS AND THAT TOWER

HIS JOB WAS UNCHANGED. DELIVERIES. From and to. Here and there. Jarred and jellied stuff, pickles and pesto from Spodosol, eggs from Proscenium Farm, greens from Brenda's Folly. Meat scraps to Victoria and Victoria's sausages to everyone including the emissaries from the Cordon, whom Journeyman met at the North Grange once a week. They sent new faces these days. Younger, mostly. The elders had declined to appear since the days of the occupation. Were they embarrassed? Or bored? Journeyman assisted Augustus, helped him murder the ducks. His rounds were familiar. He skipped the Lake of Tiredness. As with the Grange, no one new had come to live there. The path was overgrown. In time Kormentz's exile cabin would be forgotten.

Journeyman had one new client. Twice a week he crossed to the island on Astur's boat. Astur went to check on Eke and Walt; she evidently felt responsible for them. While they visited, Journeyman climbed the tower, his new backpack loaded with rations for Todbaum.

The tower's struts made a ladder. It wasn't difficult to climb except in driving rain or sharp wind. Journeyman waved his arms to scatter the crows. Having followed it from the mainland, they kept a permanent vigil atop the supercar. Never fewer than seven or eight of them there. The same ones or not, Journeyman couldn't know. Their shit streaked the chrome detailing and cockpit dome. Someday might cover it entirely. More than one had died, perhaps from the radiation, like the deer. Journeyman found the bodies at the base of the tower. One carcass had wedged into the seam where the crab claw gripped the Blue Streak's chassis. It slowly dried and dissolved until nothing remained but a few blue-black feathers. Did Todbaum encourage them with tidbits when Journeyman was gone from sight? They did seem to creep closer each time Journeyman rose to his own perch.

Todbaum dilated the portal to allow Journeyman to shove the provisions in. Journeyman had offered greetings, small inquiries, to no result. He did sometimes hear Todbaum talking to himself, a kind of bitter chortling. He didn't look good. Possibly the Blue Streak's radiation had begun to affect its pilot. Never mind his claim that the interior was lead-lined, the danger only to those outside.

Journeyman had come to take for granted the mingled stink: butane, Kahlúa, melted copper, fart. How long the Blue Streak could function in its declining state—partly crushed, tipped at an angle, never sheltered from sun or wind or the depredations of the crows—Journeyman couldn't guess. It did seem to have an inexhaustible supply of power. At night one could see its glow from the top of Tinderwick Hill. Word was it was visible as far off as Granite Head.

Todbaum never spoke, but listened. He left his door open so long as Journeyman was willing to perch on the arm of the crab-claw trap, the threshold of Todbaum's cell. Journeyman read aloud from the pages that lived in his backpack. Together they worked their way through *The Pillow Book of Jerome Kormentz*. What would they read once they'd finished? Maybe Journeyman would bring the file he'd been preparing for Drenka. Or extemporize a serial, a shaggy-dog story. *Further Adventures of the Blue Streak.* Some people liked stories in which they themselves appeared.

Having read a page of Kormentz's book, Journeyman freed it to the breeze. From the tower he could track the pages, sometimes all the way into the water. Other times they fluttered into the treetops or out of sight beyond the cliffs. Sometimes the crows, vigilant for a handout, took the bait, dive-bombed. Journeyman had more than once seen one wing off to a selfish branch to gobble a page, certain they'd gained a prize. In that sense, Journeyman felt, the white shit glazing the Blue Streak's dome could be taken as a recirculated papier-mâché art piece, a late contribution to Astur's tower. Or an encaustic form of literary criticism.

They were tired of the old stories, those birds. They wished to hear new ones.

ACKNOWLEDGMENTS

Thanks: Daniel Halpern, Zachary Wagman, Eric Simonoff, Miriam Parker, Gabriella Doob, Michael O'Connor, Kim Stanley Robinson, Chandler Klang Smith, Julie Orringer, Elvia Wilk, Steve Benson, Phil Norris, Marge Kernan, Mara Faye Lethem, Anna Moschovakis, and Dr. Neil Martinson.

And Steve Erickson, for The Intervention.